WILD AND UNBROKEN

HONEYWELLS OF KENTUCKY, BOOK 4

VANESSA GRAY BARTAL

DRY CREEK PRESS

PROLOGUE

*L*arissa Porter sat on the step and cried. She was hungry, but that was nothing new. Long ago she had given up trying to ease the gnawing ache in her belly. No, what pained her today wasn't her stomach—it was her heart.

Last year kindergarten had been so easy. Of course then she was a baby. Now she was six, practically grown up. And growing up was hard, she realized. She also realized for the first time that she wasn't like the other kids. The other kids had clothes that matched and shoes that fit. Their hair was combed. They were clean and smelled good. They packed lunches or bought food from the cafeteria. Most of them didn't have a handful of siblings at home. They arrived in shiny cars with parents who cared when they came and went.

And, as if those differences weren't bad enough, there was a difference in the way the teacher looked at her and the way she looked at the other kids, the pretty kids who hadn't had to miss a month of school because of lice. Today her beloved teacher, the one she tried so hard to love, the one she wanted to love her in return, had put her in the lowest reading group along with the boy who picked his nose and the girl who wet her pants. That was when the realization struck Larissa: her teacher thought she was stupid. And not merely stupid, but less somehow. Less than the other kids, less than good, less in every way. The realization had hurt, and the worst part was that there was no soft place to fall. Telling her parents would only earn her a smack in the mouth or, worse, their laughter.

She rested her head on her knees and wept bitterly, trying to release all her tears so she wouldn't cry on the long walk home.

"Here now, what's this?"

Larissa jumped and shied away from the speaker, even more so when she looked up to see the tall figure looming over her. Was he a grownup? Was she in trouble? But, no, when he moved out of the sunlight and sat down, she saw he was one of the Honeywells. They were all tall, almost as tall as their teachers; this one was the tallest.

She sniffled, swiping her hand over her face. He dug in his pocket, pulled out a handkerchief, and began gently scrubbing her face. Satisfied at last, he withdrew the handkerchief. Larissa cringed in embarrassment when she saw it was now black with dirt.

"Did someone hurt you?" he asked, his words soft and his tone gentle.

"Not how you suppose," she said, facing forward again. "My teacher hurt my feelings," she muttered.

"What did she do?" he asked.

"She put me in the lowest reading group. She thinks I'm stupid. I'm not stupid." She frowned, grinding her fists into her eyes to try and stop her tears before they could start again.

"Of course you're not," he said. His matter-of-fact tone surprised her. She removed her hands from her eyes and looked at him.

"How can you tell?"

He shrugged one shoulder. "Sometimes people think I'm stupid, too."

"But you're a Honeywell." The Honeywells were rich; nothing bad ever happened to them.

He smiled, shrugging again. "I'm the quiet one. People think I don't talk because I'm dumb. But I have a secret." He tapped his temple. "I don't talk because I'm smart. The surest way to show you're stupid is to open your mouth and prove it."

She blinked a few times, trying to understand his meaning. "So you think that's what I should do with my teacher? You think I should stay quiet and prove I'm smart?"

"See, you are smart. You catch on quick. I think you should work very hard until she realizes you're too smart to be in the low group. And, who knows, maybe you can help some of the other kids in that group."

She frowned in confusion again. Help other kids? That was something else she had never heard of before. In her family, everyone looked out for number one. What would it be like if she helped the nose-picking boy or the pants-peeing girl?

He stood. "Come on; I'll take you home."

"You can drive?" she asked, looking around for his car.

He laughed. "Of course not; I'm only twelve. I'll take you on my bike." He fished in his pocket again and pulled out a candy bar, holding it out to her. "Eat this on the way."

She stared at the candy in astonishment, blatant longing on her face. She had never had an entire candy bar to herself before. Usually she and her siblings fought over who would get to eat it and the biggest, roughest one won. That was almost never Larissa.

When the boy noticed she made no move to reach for the candy, he put it in her hand, curling her fingers around it. "Let's go," he said.

She walked behind him, feeling dazed. Larissa wasn't used to kindness, and especially not from one so grand as a Honeywell. Her eyes narrowed suspiciously on his back. Did he want something from her? If he did, what could it be? She had nothing to give.

He straddled his bike and lifted her up onto the handlebars as easily as if she were a baby. "Don't be scared," he commanded.

"I'm not scared," she said sincerely. And she wasn't; she was awed and exhilarated, especially when he took off and sent her long hair flying behind her in ribbons.

All too soon it was over. They reached her house and he lifted her down. "Goodbye, little Porter," he said.

Larissa frowned, not sure why it should bother her that he knew without being told that she was a Porter. "Which Honeywell are you?" she asked.

"I'm Everett," he said. He hopped on his bike and took off, never looking back. Larissa stood in front of her house and watched him until he faded from view.

CHAPTER 1

"Unit fifty."

"Unit fifty, go ahead."

"Unit fifty, we have a report of a code twenty in front of Penny's café."

"Clear." Larissa pushed the button on her lapel and started her car, turning in the direction of Penny's when her dispatcher, Melody, spoke again, less formally this time.

"It's the Honeywells. Again."

Larissa stopped the cruiser and pinched the bridge of her nose. Not the Honeywells, not tonight. *Please don't let it be Everett,* she prayed, but she was almost certain it would be. Now that his older three brothers were happily settled and domesticated, Everett and Grant seemed to be the only two who got into trouble. Sure enough, when she pulled to a stop in front of Penny's café, the first person she saw was Everett Honeywell, though, to his credit, he wasn't the one on the ground brawling. Instead he stood back, arms crossed, looking almost bored by the scene, but Larissa wasn't fooled. She knew there was more going on behind his placid expression than met the eye; she had learned the hard way.

She erupted from her cruiser and stopped short in front of the fray on the ground. There was a tangle of limbs, but some of them seemed to belong to Grant Honeywell. The other person was an unknown, but whoever he was, he was losing the fight. Badly.

"Stop," she called. When the men wrestling on the sidewalk paid her no mind, she tried again, louder this time, but still they didn't stop pounding each other. She took a breath, trying not to sigh at the knowledge that she was about to dive into the tangle of bodies. But before she could take the plunge, Everett reached down and plucked his brother and the other man apart, holding them far away from each other with his long arms. Grant Honeywell looked no worse the wear, but the other man was a mess. His shirt was untucked, his nose was bleeding, and his hair resembled a bird's nest.

He struggled against Everett's iron grip for a few seconds until he caught sight of Larissa. "Officer, arrest that man," he implored, pointing at Grant.

Grant didn't reply, but he did jump at the man, making him shrink away in terror. Everett let his brother go, and they both faced Larissa.

"What's going on here?' she asked, looking between the three men, all of whom towered over her, but none so much as Everett.

"He hit me for nothing," the man said.

"He kicked his dog," Grant said, pointing to the ground behind Larissa. She turned, noticing the dog for the first time. Indeed, he lay on the ground looking injured and pathetic.

She whirled on the man, frowning. "Did you kick your dog, sir?"

"So what if I did?" he answered belligerently. "It's my dog. No crime against punishing it."

Grant started to speak, but Larissa held up her hand, cutting him off. "Actually, there is," she contradicted.

"Still doesn't give him the right to hit me," he said, glaring at Grant.

Larissa turned to look questioningly at Grant. "Did you hit him?" she asked.

"I gave him the chance to apologize to the dog," Grant said.

"Who apologizes to dogs?" the man yelled.

"People who kick them," Grant said. He turned back to Larissa. "Look, officer," he glanced at her nametag. "Porter." He paused, cocking his head to the side. "There's a Porter who's a cop? I didn't know that."

"You were telling me why you hit him," she said, trying to get him back on track.

"Right. I hit him because he kicked the dog and wouldn't apologize. I gave him fair warning."

"Mr. Honeywell," she began in a longsuffering tone. "I appreciate that you don't like to see animals mistreated, but you cannot go around hitting men when it happens."

"Why not?" he asked as the other man snickered.

"And you," she turned her attention on the man whom she was disliking more and more, "cannot kick your dog."

"I can if I want to. It's my dog. Now I want him arrested." Once again he glared at Grant.

"I didn't do anything wrong," Grant said. "I gave you fair warning. It's not my fault you're too stubborn or too stupid to apologize."

They would have gone at each other again, but Larissa inserted herself between them, pressing her palms on their chests. "Stop it," she yelled. They paused, looking at her. "Both of you are under arrest."

"What?" the man exploded, shaking free of her grasp. "You're taking his side because he's a Honeywell."

"I'm not taking anyone's side; that's not my job. My job is to uphold the law, and from where I stand, you've both broken it," Larissa said calmly.

"You think you can arrest me?" the man said, advancing on her. "You little…" Whatever he might have said was cut off as Everett once again laid a restraining hand on his shoulder.

"The officer said you're under arrest," Everett said. "I suggest you put your arms behind your back now."

The man complied, clearly seething the entire time. Larissa cuffed him and then cuffed Grant Honeywell who dutifully held his arms in the same manner.

"You can put yours in front," she told him. "I only do the back if the suspect is uncooperative."

Grant smiled at her and moved his arms to the front. "You can't tell me he didn't deserve a fat lip for kicking his dog," he whispered.

"Unfortunately, I can't give my opinion on a matter that's for the court," Larissa said. She led both men to the back of her cruiser, instructing them not to talk to each other so no more arguments would ensue on the way to the jail. After closing them in the cruiser, she slammed the door and stalked back to Everett who stood staring at her in utter amusement.

She stopped short in front of him.

"Officer Porter," he said politely, pretending to tip an imaginary hat.

Larissa fisted her hands on her hips and glared. "I did not need your help with that," she hissed.

"That's not what it looked like to me," he said mildly.

"It is not up to you to interfere in police business, no matter what your opinion is. You are a civilian."

"Yes ma'am," he said dutifully.

She scowled, not in the mood for his condescension. "I can handle myself. If I couldn't, I wouldn't be an officer."

"If you say so," he said. Turning his attention to the poor, injured dog lying on the ground, he bent and gently scooped it up, ignoring the dog when it growled at him. "Looks like you two have a lot in common," he said.

"Are you comparing me to a dog?" she asked, aghast.

"Not necessarily. I'm simply pointing out that you both growl at the hand that's trying to help you."

Larissa could feel her temper about to explode. She forced herself to take a deep breath and remain professional. "What are you going to do with the dog?"

"I'm going to take him to my brother. I think some ribs are broken."

"Please ask your brother to document the animal's injuries; I may need them for court."

"Yes, ma'am," Everett said.

"And stop calling me ma'am," she snapped before returning to the driver's side of her car.

"I could call you sweetheart, but it doesn't seem appropriate," Everett called.

"Don't call me anything," she said, slamming into her car and driving away.

CHAPTER 2

"Do you know my brother?" Grant asked as soon as Larissa slid behind the wheel of her cruiser.

"What makes you ask?" she said, hedging.

"I've never seen him talk so much to a stranger before, even a pretty one."

"Your brother and I go way back," she said vaguely, giving no hint of the detailed and humiliating history that she and Everett Honeywell shared. Somehow it didn't surprise her that he hadn't seen fit to tell his family about her.

"Are you a Porter by birth, or did you marry one?" Grant asked.

In his eyes, she wasn't sure which would be worse. "Birth," she said, hoping her crisp tone would turn away any further questions.

"Where do you fall in line?"

"I'm in the middle." Before he could ask, she provided the answer to his next question. "I was five years behind you in school."

"You're only twenty three?" he exclaimed.

She glared at him in the rearview mirror.

"I mean, not that you look old," he backpedaled. "It's that I don't usually think of police officers as being so much younger than me.

You seem very authoritative and sure of yourself for someone so young."

"I've been a cop for four years now," she said, relaxing as they transitioned from her family to her job.

"Four years," Grant repeated, impressed. "I admire ambition."

The other man in the back seat snickered. Grant turned to him with a scowl. "What's your problem?" he asked.

"Nothing at all, I'm enjoying this little love fest," the man said, his tone derisive.

"It's called being polite," Grant said. "Though I wouldn't expect anyone who would kick a dog to understand."

"Fellas," Larissa said, intercepting before another fight could explode. The tension in the back seat was palpable, but unless the culprits were drunk or high a sharp word was usually enough to get things back under control again. "Either of you on anything?" Though she couldn't say it out loud, she was referring to the unknown man sitting behind her. The Honeywells were notorious non-drinkers.

"No," Grant said. "Unless you count sweet tea as a drug."

"What about you, sir?" Larissa addressed her attention to the other man.

"I had a couple of beers with lunch, but I wasn't driving," he added caustically. "You can't arrest me for that."

Larissa fought the temptation to roll her eyes. The chip on his shoulder was a mile wide. If she had to guess, she would say he was probably a regular with law enforcement, though she didn't recognize him. "Where are you from?" she asked.

"Frankfort, and I'm going back there as soon as I get out of jail and collect my dog," the man said.

"You can't have your dog," Grant said hotly.

"You can't keep my dog from me; he's mine," the man said.

Larissa held up her hand. "Gentlemen, let's have silence until we arrive at the jail which will be in exactly two minutes."

They complied. Grant sat back, a placid smile on his face, while the other man turned to look sullenly out his window, his brow lowered in anger or disgust. Maybe both.

Larissa arrived at the jail and waited for the sally port to be opened. Once inside, she let the jailers take over directing her prisoners from the car. After she saw them safely inside, she left them, going to the patrol room to write her report. The report took so long that it was quitting time by the time she was finished. She hurriedly filed it and headed toward her car, not realizing someone was calling her name until she was almost there.

"Officer Porter."

Tensing, she turned until she saw it was Grant Honeywell, and then she relaxed. "You made bail already?" she blurted.

He nodded. "We sort of have the routine down pat by now. I was hoping I would run into you. Um, I know this is bad timing and all since you arrested me, but would you maybe want to go out sometime?"

"It really is bad timing," Larissa said, smiling to soften the blow she was about to deliver. "I'm not allowed to date anyone I've arrested. I could get fired."

"Oh," he said. He sounded disappointed for only a fraction of an instant, and then it was over and his happy smile was back in place. "Have a nice evening."

"You, too," she said. Turning once again toward her car, she stepped inside and cranked the ignition. Nothing happened. *Not now,* she pled, frantically trying again and again to make the engine crank. "No, no, no!" she yelled out loud, banging her fist on the steering wheel. She had forgotten that Grant Honeywell was there until he opened her door and stuck his head inside.

"Won't start, huh?"

She shook her head, frustrated beyond speech.

"I'm not the world's best mechanic, but I'll take a look if you want."

Larissa remained seated in the car, debating with herself about the ethics of having someone she had arrested fix her vehicle. Finally, desperation won over ethics. She *had* to get home. "That would be great, thanks." She followed him to the front of the car and stood by while he popped the hood. "Aren't you an engineer?"

He quirked an eyebrow at her in surprise. "Not many people outside my family know that."

She shrugged, looking awkwardly away, not wanting to reveal how much she knew about his family. "Word spreads," she said vaguely.

"Yes, well, unfortunately this is beyond my expertise. I'm sorry to say I think your transmission is shot. Looks like you've been leaking fluid for a while now."

"I've been meaning to take it in," she said. Money and time had both prevented her from doing so, but there was no need to pour out her problems on Grant's overly large shoulders. She didn't want to be beholden to any of the Honeywells for anything ever again, but to make matters worse, the quiet purr of an SUV sounded as they finished their conversation. Everett rolled up in one of the family's fleet of vehicles. No one could ever tell how many cars they had because they were all large and black, nearly indistinguishable from each other. But she thought each brother had his own car and then there were a couple of business vehicles, and the parents owned a car or two. At least they always made a point of buying local, much to the area car dealer's immense satisfaction.

"What's going on?" Everett asked as he unfolded himself from his car. No matter how large the cars were, they never seemed to be large enough to encompass the Honeywells. On the rare occasions they all rode together it was like watching a clown car on steroids as a never-ending stream of too-tall brothers poured out.

"Her car won't start," Grant informed him. Larissa shifted uncomfortably and tried to look anywhere but at Everett. "I was about to offer her a ride."

"Thanks, but I can't ride with you," Larissa said, trying to infuse the proper amount of gratitude into her tone. The last thing she wanted was a ride from them.

"No problem," Grant said, unruffled. "I'll wait here for the tow and Everett can run you home. You didn't arrest him," he pointed out.

"Oh, I, uh…" she fumbled about, searching for an excuse, any excuse to get out of spending even a minute alone with Everett. He knew, of course, and smiled at her discomfort. Irritated, she finally acquiesced. Now that the idea was hatched, there was no way to get out of it. "Okay," she said at last, glaring up at Everett who returned her look with a patronizing smile. "Thank you," she added sincerely to Grant.

His return smile was warm and genuine. She hoped his legal troubles would work themselves out. Though she couldn't admit it to him, she was on his side. The drunken loser had deserved a fat lip and then some for kicking his poor dog.

Everett didn't try to help her into the vehicle, probably knowing she would never allow it. But the fact that he hadn't even tried was a strike against him, even though it would have been a strike against him if he had tried, too.

"I live…" she started, but he interrupted, cutting her off.

"I know where you live."

There were a couple minutes of awkward silence. She was loathe to break it, but she was also curious about the dog. "How's the dog?"

"A couple of broken ribs and a whole lot of bruising. Darcy says this wasn't his first injury, too."

Larissa clucked her tongue. "Stupid fool," she muttered.

"Me or the dog's owner?" Everett asked with his usual dry amusement.

Larissa didn't answer. They reached her tiny rental house and she hopped out of the tall car, practically at a sprint. "Thank you," she called over her shoulder. But there was no need; Everett was right behind her. "What are you doing?"

"I'm seeing you inside. Don't argue," he added, preempting her inevitable argument. He opened her door for her and she gritted her teeth, knowing that to protest would be futile.

"Let me go first," she said, sidestepping him when he started to enter the door. "You'll scare him."

There was a clatter of dishes and then the joyful sound of her son's voice. "Mommy!" He ran at her full tilt from the kitchen, arms outstretched. "I made you a surprise!"

"Owen, were you cooking? You know you're not supposed to," Larissa said, hating that discipline had to be her first response to him.

"I didn't turn on the stove," he said, shaking his head. "I mixed some stuff together."

"I can't wait to see," she said, feigning enthusiasm while she wondered what horrid combination she was going to have to choke down. She enfolded him in her arms, hugging as tightly as he would allow. After he was properly hugged, he released his mother and stepped back, craning his neck to survey Everett from head to toe.

"Who's he?" Owen asked.

"This is Mr. Honeywell," Larissa explained.

"Hello," Owen said, half in awe as he held out his little hand for a shake.

Everett smiled, his return shake swallowing the boy's hand whole. "How do you do, Owen?"

"I'm fine, sir," he said. Having decided Everett was of no further importance, he once again turned his attention to his mother. "Can I go get my surprise?"

Larissa nodded, watching him with a smile as he scurried away.

Everett's smile disappeared as soon as Owen did. "You leave him alone here while you work?"

Larissa looked up at him, her eyes flashing fire. "Don't judge me. He's in school most of the day and he's only alone for about an hour."

"He's seven, Lissa. That's too young to be left by himself."

"Don't lecture me about my son, and don't call me that."

"Why not?" he asked.

"Because he's my son," she snapped.

"I meant the name. You never minded before."

"Well I mind now," she said.

"Still, you know what I'm saying is true. He's too young to be left alone here for any length of time."

She blew out a breath, barely containing her fury. "Don't you think I know that?" she asked through gritted teeth. "But what am I supposed to do? Leave him with my family?" She snorted an indelicate laugh. "He'd be better off on the street. And I can't find a sitter that will work for such a short length of time, not one that I trust, anyway."

He narrowed his eyes thoughtfully as he looked toward the kitchen. "Leave him with us," he said.

"No," Larissa said, not even considering it.

"We can arrange for the bus to drop him at the farm and we'll watch him until you get off work," he reiterated, as if she hadn't understood him the first time.

"No," she repeated.

"You know he'll be safe with me and my brothers. And kids love the farm. Working with the horses will be great for him."

"No," she reiterated, not even giving in to the temptation to think about such a proposition.

"Lissa," Everett said, his tone turning stern and parental. "Don't let your stubbornness ruin something for your son. You know it's better for him to be with us than to be alone. What if you can't get home in time? What if you get injured on the job and no one knows where he is? What if…"

She couldn't let him continue to list the fears she had already thought of for herself. "Stop it," she said through gritted teeth and closed eyes. "Please stop. Owen is not your responsibility; he's mine, and I'm doing a good job with him."

"No one is saying you aren't, but everyone needs help now and then. The farm is ideal for little boys; I should know because I was a little boy there. He'll love it, he'll be safe, and it will be a weight off your shoulders."

"Don't say you're doing it for me," she said. "I don't need your help."

He didn't reply. He simply looked at her, waiting for her stubborn refusal to die down until she gave in and did things his way. Oh, how she wanted to keep on fighting. But he was right; going to the Honeywell farm was a much better proposition for Owen than spending his afternoons alone in their ramshackle house in their rundown neighborhood. Everyone knew he was alone, making him a target for her family or neighbors who had ill intentions. Who was she kidding—he was a sitting duck and going to the Honeywells after school was a dream come true. All she had to do was swallow years worth of pride and allow it.

"That would be very kind of you," she said at last, choking on the words.

Owen returned then with a suspicious-looking bowl in hand. "Owen, Mr. Honeywell has asked if you would like to spend your afternoons at his farm. He and his family live in that big farm that you're always asking me about."

"No way, you live there?" Owen asked, his eyes round with excitement.

"I do, and we've been looking for someone about your age to help us with the horses. Are you interested? Before you answer, let me warn you that it's not easy work. We need someone strong."

"I'm strong," Owen said, nodding. "I can do it, mister."

"You can call me Everett." He smiled. "What have you got in that bowl?"

Owen peered in his bowl. "Some cereal, peanut butter, ketchup, an egg, and a whole bunch of spices I found in the cabinet."

"You're mom is real lucky to have you to cook for her," Everett said, turning a beaming smile on Larissa.

"Owen, sweetheart, we're being rude. Why don't you offer Mr. Honeywell a bite?" Larissa said, her tone dripping honey.

"Sure," Owen said, holding out his bowl to Everett. "I haven't tasted it yet, so the spoon is clean."

"Okay," Everett said, and Larissa had to give him credit for sounding cheerful. He picked up the spoon and took a large bite, smiling as he chewed. "I think you have a real talent for creativity in the kitchen, Owen. It's your mom's turn now." He scooped an even larger bite and shoved it in Larissa's mouth, watching in amusement while she fought her gag reflex.

"Someone found the cayenne," she said, swiping the tears from her lashes.

"What's that?" Owen asked.

"It's a hot pepper," Larissa said, sniffling to contain her runny nose.

"Oh," Owen said, his tone disappointed as he stared into his bowl.

"But Everett's right, you're really creative in the kitchen. Maybe we can check out some cookbooks from the library and cook together," Larissa suggested.

"That would be awesome," Owen said with his usual enthusiasm.

Larissa knew Everett was watching, soaking in every word like a washcloth. He was an avid observer of people, but he seemed especially interested in her interaction with her son. She wondered if he was judging her, trying to see if she was raising him the way she had been raised. Or rather, the way she hadn't been raised. Her upbringing was practically feral.

"Sweetheart, say goodbye to Mr. Honeywell. You'll see him tomorrow," Larissa said.

"Goodbye, Mr. Honeywell," Owen said dutifully as he glanced up from his bowl.

"Goodbye, Owen. I look forward to knowing you better."

Larissa frowned, not liking that proposition at all. "Why don't you take your bowl back to the kitchen? I'll be in soon."

Owen nodded, wandering toward the kitchen, bowl in hand.

"Do you need a ride to work tomorrow?" Everett asked. "There's no way your car will be ready in time."

Larissa shook her head, hating that she had to be grateful and polite again. "No, thank you, I'll be fine."

Everett studied her, probably trying to read her mind. "You've changed, Lissy."

"I've grown up, Everett. I'm not the same starry-eyed, needy kid I was."

"Hmm. I'm not sure, but I think I liked you better before. Lock this door when I leave." With that, he turned and swept regally from the room.

Of course you liked me better before, Larissa thought, dutifully locking the door because it's what she would have done anyway. *I adored you, and you knew it.* She shook her head, trying to dislodge thoughts of Everett, but he was like a bug that had crawled inside her brain to nest. For the last few years, she had been able to put him out of her mind and focus on Owen. But today's interaction had dislodged old thoughts and memories, bringing them to the surface to torture her again.

Time and again she had made a fool of herself in front of Everett Honeywell, had been dependent on him for her very survival. But no more. She was a capable adult now with a son to support, and she would die before she would be dependent on Everett or any other man ever again.

CHAPTER 3

Larissa stood looking at the candy display, her mouth watering. One candy bar in particular jumped out at her; it was the same kind Everett Honeywell had given her two years ago. She hadn't eaten one like it since that day, but she hadn't forgotten the taste. She was so hungry. Was it really so wrong to simply reach out and take one? To stuff it in her pocket and walk calmly out of the store as she had seen her brothers, sisters, and even parents do so many times?

For the last two years, Larissa had tried to be good. Somehow, though her parents had never told her, she knew stealing was wrong, the same way she knew lying was wrong. But her family never had money to buy things besides beer, cigarettes, and lottery tickets. The cupboards were always bare, her clothes were always torn. She wanted to have nice things like the other kids. She wanted to have lots of food to eat. She wanted her hair to be clean and not smell like cigarettes, but there was no shampoo or soap at her house, either. Larissa knew she was supposed to use those things because the nurse at school had told her so, even giving her a small bottle of good-smelling stuff. But as soon as Larissa arrived home with it, her older sister had swiped it for herself and Larissa never saw it again.

She was so tired of being different. At school, she was different because she was too much like her family. Kids thought she was dirty and poor by choice. But at home she didn't fit in, either. She didn't want to be like her family. She wanted to be cleaner, richer, better. She didn't want to smoke or drink or scream or curse all the time. She didn't want to steal. Today, however, Larissa was learning that there was a vast difference between good intentions and reality. She didn't want to steal, but she felt like she was starving. What would it hurt if she took one candy bar? Mr. Hampton, the store's owner, was as rich as Moses. He wouldn't care if she took one, would he?

Convinced that it was the only way, Larissa grabbed the candy bar in her fist. She tucked the first edge into her pocket when a steely hand clamped around her wrist. Panicked, she looked up, expecting to see Mr. Hampton or the police. But it was someone much worse. It was Everett Honeywell.

"What are you doing?" he hissed, his tone and expression dripping disapproval.

"I..." Larissa began as shades of humiliation and shame flushed over her face. "I want...I'm so hungry." With that, she dropped the candy bar and burst into tears. She would have run out of the store, but Everett hadn't lessened his grip on her wrist.

He sighed, bending forward to pick up the candy bar. "We're going to go to the front of the store. You're going to confess to Mr. Hampton about what almost happened, and you're going to apologize. Do you understand?"

Larissa nodded, trying hard to swallow her misery and her tears. She allowed Everett to lead her forward to the front of the store. He stood beside her, giving her a slight nudge when she was reluctant to speak. "I was going to steal a candy bar, but Everett stopped me. I'm sorry," she whispered, swiping her face with her sleeve.

Mr. Hampton sighed in the same way Everett had sighed, as if he had expected as much but was disappointed nonetheless. "Larissa, I know your brothers and sisters steal from me, and even your parents sometimes. I also know that you've never stolen from me before. I've had high hopes for you, and I don't want to see you turn out like them. Do you understand what I'm saying? I expect better behavior from you. You're a good girl."

She blinked up at him in surprise, squinting hard to see him through her tear-wet lashes. He thought she was a good girl? Her, a Porter? "Yes, sir," she whispered. "I'm sorry."

He nodded. "Let's not have a repeat of this again. I always know what goes on in my store."

She shivered, swiping the back of her hand over her nose as she nodded. Everett produced a tissue from his pocket and handed it to her. When she was done wiping her nose, he clasped her hand and led her to the door, stopping short before they went outside.

He let go her hand and settled his hands on her shoulders, looking into her eyes. "That was a good thing you did. Everyone makes mistakes sometimes; the real test of who you are is what you do about them. You admitted your mistake and apologized, and that's good. Do you understand?"

She nodded. The ugly weight in her chest had eased some with her admission, and she understood how making things right was the proper thing to do.

Everett smiled. "Good girl. Now I want you to go back in the store and pick out whatever you want. It's my treat."

"Oh," Larissa said, not sure how to respond to the unexpected turn of events. A part of her felt like she should refuse the gift, but she didn't understand that part of her. He was offering to buy her things, why should she refuse? Without further delay, she turned on her heel and went back to the candy aisle. But when she stared at the candy bar now she had lost her taste for it. The trauma of almost stealing and being caught had cured her of her desire for chocolate and sugar.

Instead she left the candy aisle and went to the personal care aisle, a place she had rarely visited with her family. What had the nurse said she should do every day? Wash with soap, use shampoo on her hair, and brush her teeth.

Larissa owned a toothbrush because the dentist who came to school gave her one. But there was no toothpaste in the house, so she didn't often use it. Today she chose a box of toothpaste, a bottle of shampoo that smelled like strawberries, and a bar of Ivory soap. There were lots of soaps, but she liked how Ivory was white. Nothing in Larissa's house was white, nothing looked so pure.

When she returned to Everett with the soap, shampoo, and toothpaste in her arms, his mouth opened slightly in surprise as he took in her selections. He cleared his throat, blinking rapidly as he looked away from her. Larissa frowned. Did he disapprove? Would he say no? But, no, he didn't refuse. He put his hand on her back, urging her toward the counter, and then he grabbed a jar of peanut butter and the cursed candy bar, adding them to her items.

Mr. Hampton and Everett exchanged a long look, one that Larissa didn't understand, but one that made both of them clear their throats and blink a whole bunch again. Maybe it was a grown-up thing. Everett was fourteen now; that was practically full grown. Mr. Hampton said the total out loud, and Larissa's heart sank. It was so much, she was sure Everett would tell her to put some things back. But he didn't. Instead he pulled out his wallet and paid, using only a small portion of bills from the giant stack in his wallet.

Suddenly Larissa's resentment rose to the surface again. It wasn't fair that his family had so much and hers had so little. No wonder Everett could smell good and be well fed. His family had lots of money. If hers had that much money, they might love her and feed her, too.

Everett took the bag and Larissa followed him outside. Her sullenness over glimpsing his money had made her forget to say thank you, so she amended that now. "Thank you, Everett," she said.

He sat on the curb, patting the pavement beside him. Larissa sat down and they stared over the parking lot. "Do you know why I have money?" he asked.

Larissa frowned. Could he read her mind? It certainly seemed that way. "'Cause you were born that way," she said, some of her resentment leaking into her tone.

"That's my parents' money. I have money because I work hard for it and they pay me, like any stable hand. I muck stalls—that means I shovel heavy piles of manure, every afternoon for a few hours. On Saturdays, I bathe the horses and comb them. I earn my money; I don't get it for free."

Larissa nodded, feeling more charitable towards him again. She had smelled horse manure before, and she didn't envy anyone who had to shovel it. "But how can I earn money? I'm only a kid."

"By earning good grades," Everett said.

"I already earn good grades," Larissa said proudly. Two years ago in first grade, she had risen from the lowest to the highest reading group. Since then she had been at the top of her class.

"Prove it. Bring me your report card and for every A you earn, I'll give you money."

"You'll give me money for my grades?" Larissa repeated, stunned. As far as she could tell, no one could care less if she passed or failed school. In fact, her family seemed to resent her good marks, calling her names whenever she brought home A's. She had learned to keep a low profile on report card day.

Everett nodded. "Two dollars for every A."

"Two dollars," Larissa exclaimed, doing the calculation in her head. *"That's fourteen dollars a grade card."*

"Only if you earn all A's," Everett said.

"I will," Larissa said, determination causing her to frown.

"Good," Everett said. Larissa thought the conversation was at an end, but he turned to her, and earnest expression on his face. *"I want you to be good, Lissy."*

"It's Larissa," she said, disappointed that he had forgotten her name.

"I know. It's a nickname, something people give each other when they're friends."

She nodded, trying to take in the fact that he thought of her as a friend. To her, he was more angel than friend. *"I'll try,"* she said.

"You can always come to me if you need anything. You know that, don't you?"

She nodded, though she didn't mean it. Everett had a knack for showing up when she needed him, but she couldn't picture herself ever going to him at his family's pristine farm. She would sully it by being near it. *"And you can come to me if you need something,"* she added because it was the polite thing to say and because it made her feel good to make the offer.

Everett nodded solemnly as if thinking that over. *"I might. You take care, and be good."* He stressed the last two words. Larissa turned them over in her mind, trying to figure out if she even knew what it meant to be good. Not stealing was a start. She promised herself that, no matter how hungry she became, she would never steal again.

CHAPTER 4

"**B**ut, Mom, I already made supper," Owen said, his tone wheedling.

"Owen, I appreciate the fact that you went to so much trouble. But we can't eat raw eggs, honey. We could get sick."

"Oh."

Larissa hated the disappointment in his little face. "Why don't you set the table and after supper we'll go out and play some ball?"

"Okay," he said, his face lighting again.

Larissa smiled, enjoying how easy it was to make him happy. Sometimes the same thought made her sad for the little girl she had been. It would have taken so little effort for her parents to pour one ounce of care into her, but they hadn't. She sighed, letting it go again. It did no good to dwell on her childhood; it was over, and she had thrived despite their neglect. Owen may not have a father, but at least he had her, and she gave him all the love, care, and training she had lacked as a child.

Owen set the table while Larissa sautéed chicken breasts and vegetables. When she was Owen's age, the only vegetables she ate had been at school. Like most other areas of their lives, she overcompensated now, providing Owen with meals that would make any dietician happy.

"Mom, who was that man?" Owen asked as they began their meal. Larissa wanted to sigh and put her head on the table, but that might alert Owen to the fact that Everett had some special significance in her life. Instead, she tried to keep her answer vague and her tone casual.

"He's a man I've known for a long time."

"When you were little like me?"

"When I was about your age," she said. "His family is very nice; you'll like them."

He stared at his plate for a while, thinking. Larissa braced herself for what might come next. The more time Owen spent thinking up a question, the more complex it was going to be.

"Is he my dad?"

Nothing could have braced her for that one. Larissa choked, even though there was no food in her mouth, and took a swallow of water before answering. "Owen, what makes you ask that?"

"You've known him for a long time and we sort of look alike."

Leave it to Owen to pick up on that. "No, honey, he is not your dad. He's someone I used to know."

"Maybe he could be my dad and then I could have a little brother," Owen suggested.

Larissa set down her fork and removed her hand to her lap so she could clutch it into a fist without her son knowing. "Owen, that's not going to happen. I know you want a dad, and I'd like that for you, too. But dads aren't made that way. If I ever get married, it's going to have to be someone we both love, someone who fits into our family and makes it better. That's a tall order."

"Everett is tall," Owen pointed out.

"You're very literal," Larissa said, smiling. "I didn't mean I want someone tall. I meant it would take a special person to be all the things we need. Everett is being nice by letting you visit his farm, but that's not reason enough to try and make him your dad."

Owen sighed, visibly disappointed. Larissa bit back her own disappointment, too. No matter how hard she tried to be all things to her son, she couldn't be a father to him, not really. They could play ball, watch sports, or go hiking, but it wasn't the same as having a man in his life. If she knew what that one glaring mistake would have cost her, she still wouldn't undo it because then she wouldn't have Owen. But the weight of guilt for her bad choice still rested heavily on her head.

After supper, Larissa cleaned up while Owen sat on the counter and talked to her. She could have stayed in the kitchen all night, scrubbing and disinfecting things. After the chaos and grit of her childhood, she tended to go overboard on cleaning, but she forced herself to put down the disinfectant and take Owen outside. Grabbing the ball on her way out the door, they stood in their miniscule front yard, throwing back and forth. Before Owen, Larissa had no idea how to catch or receive a football. Like many things she had taught him to do, she had looked it up on the internet and taught herself first. Now she had a vast knowledge of all sports involving a ball, fishing, and trains. Owen was turning out to be a guy's guy, and she didn't want him to miss out on manly things because there wasn't a man in his life.

They tossed the ball back and forth for a while. Maybe she was biased, but Larissa thought Owen was good at both passing and throwing. Soon she would need to sign him up for pee wee football, but she had no idea where she would find the time or money, especially with her car now broken. She had to stop thinking about it, or she would feel like she was drowning. Single parenthood was not for the faint of heart.

"All right, buddy, that's enough. It's bath time."

"Aw, Mom," Owen complained. "I don't need a bath. I had a bath last night."

"You need a bath every night," she said. Her sweet son had no idea what a luxury a bath was. When she was younger, their bathtub had been filled with trash. Larissa had bathed herself in the sink as best she could, hiding her soap, shampoo, and toothpaste in a bag under her bed so her siblings wouldn't steal it. Not that they would have used it. No, they couldn't stand to see someone possess something they didn't have.

The first time Larissa ever took a full shower was in the hospital after she had Owen. She didn't enlighten Owen, though. She had made it a rule never to begin a sentence with, "When I was your age…" It was bad enough that she had the nightmares of her childhood in her mind; there was no need to burden Owen with that information.

She sat in the bathroom while he bathed himself and played in the water, taking special care to rinse the shampoo from his hair when he was ready to get out. She tucked him into bed and read two stories before saying his prayers and giving him a kiss. Slowly, she backed out of the room, leaving the door cracked so the hall light could filter in.

At last it was her chance to unwind. She loved Owen, but this small pause between his bedtime and hers was her only break each day, her only chance to be Larissa and not Officer Porter or Owen's mom. Not that she had much chance to relax. She needed to run a load of laundry, fold another, pack Owen's lunch, pay a couple of bills, balance her checkbook, pack her own lunch, and lay out her own clothes for the next day. And it helped matters if she set out their bowls and cereal boxes, too. Mornings were hectic. As much as she could get accomplished before bed was less to do while trying to get them out the door. Usually she had a few minutes after Owen left for school, but tomorrow she would need every minute because she would have to ride her bike to work. But at least she wouldn't have to work out. Unfortunately her workouts were few and far between, even though she was contractually obligated to stay in good shape for her job. Occasionally she managed a quick run on the bike path while Owen rode his bike beside her, but those times were fewer and farther between now that he was in school fulltime.

There was more that needed doing, but Larissa had long ago learned that something always needed to be done. Putting aside her checkbook, she picked up the fiction book she had been trying to read for the last month. Finding her place took a moment because Owen had knocked it from the stool, losing her bookmark. At last she found the correct page and began to read.

An unknown time later, she woke sitting upright in the chair, the book having toppled to the floor. She sighed. So much for reading. Instead she went to the bathroom and took a long, hot shower—her second that day. Showers were her one indulgent luxury and she often took two or three a day. But no matter how many she took, she could never completely remove the traces of the dirty little girl she had been, nor the shame from all the years of living in squalor. When she finished, she generously slathered her skin with lotion, reminding herself once again that she wouldn't need so much lotion if she didn't take so many showers. She ran a comb through her long, auburn hair, climbed between the sheets and fell asleep.

When her alarm woke her, she thought it was a mistake, but then she always did. There was no rest for the weary, apparently. Groggily, she pulled herself out of bed and made her way to Owen's room. He woke easier than she did, thanks to his eleven hours of sleep, and she began the routine of nudging him to readiness. Like any seven year old boy, he was easily distracted. Larissa spent half her morning reminding him to do what she had already told him to do, namely to get dressed and brush his teeth. Today he seemed especially sluggish, so she decided to up the ante after the third time she told him to hurry up.

"If you get dressed in the next three minutes, then I'll let you watch television for a few minutes until your bus arrives."

Television, something he was so rarely allowed to watch, worked like a magic inducement so that he was dressed with his hair combed, teeth brushed, and sitting at the breakfast table in less than two minutes. They ate cereal together and then he plopped in front of the television while Larissa stuffed his lunch into his backpack, zipped it up, and set it beside him on the floor.

She braided her hair, as was her standard routine for work. She supposed she should cut it so as not to give suspects a handhold if she got in a fight, but the thought of cutting off all her hair was somehow traumatizing. Instead she kept it out of the way, even occasionally remembering to tuck the end of the braid into her shirt if she felt like she might become involved in a confrontation.

Her watch beeped, alerting her to the fact that it was time for Owen to stand outside for the bus. He was staring mesmerized at the television, reminding her again why she limited the time he was allowed to watch. Was he even blinking? She turned it off and he slowly came back to life, looking at her in mutinous protest.

"Time for the bus," she said before he could complain.

He sighed, standing to retrieve his book bag. She kissed him before they went outside, knowing he would die a thousand deaths if she kissed him goodbye in front of the school bus.

"Have a good day, buddy," she said.

"You, too, Mom," he said, sounding so much like a grownup that she smiled.

The bus arrived almost as soon as they stepped onto the porch. She watched until he was safely inside and then she went back to the house, gathered her own bag and took her bicycle from the closet.

With a sigh, she hopped on the bike and began to pedal. There had been too many days over the last few years when riding her bike had been a necessity. To say her car was unreliable was an understatement. But how was she supposed to afford a new one when she could barely afford anything else? She was still paying her college loans, eking out their monthly rent and utilities, and trying to get by on what was left over. Sometimes she wished for someone to tell her what to do in life. She could move to Lexington and make better money, but then she would be living in the big city, and that frightened her for Owen's sake. At least here in Silver Springs she might make barely enough to live on, but she knew everyone Owen came in contact with. Grimacing, she realized that the worst this town had to offer was her very own family. Ironically, they were the people she feared the most. Owen had met his relatives, of course, but only from a safe distance and at a time when they were least likely to be drunk or high.

Miraculously, Larissa hadn't had to arrest one of her siblings yet. Not that they hadn't been in trouble with the law, because they had, but somehow they always managed to contain their mischief to the nighttime, and Larissa worked days. Her parents, thankfully, seemed to have grown into law-abiding citizens. Old before their time, they preferred staying home, watching television, and getting drunk in the privacy of their living room. Unlike when Larissa had been little and they had gone out most evenings, cruising the bars and getting arrested for drunk driving or fighting—sometimes with each other, and sometimes with other people.

She would never understand her family, but how could she? They seemed to have their own unknown code that made sense to no one but them. Her parents, for instance, fought like crazy but had been married for thirty years. Divorce wasn't an option for them, but domestic violence was. Her siblings, with the exception of herself, were mean and hateful, but they were all close to each other, spending birthdays and holidays together. Granted someone usually ended up in jail on those days, but they spent them together nonetheless. She was seen as the holier-than-thou outcast, derided by all, hated by some. Only her parents had a grudging acceptance of her and they were surprisingly nice to Owen on the rare occasions they saw him.

"Shades of gray," she muttered. Her family was neither black nor white, but somewhere in the middle. Lawless but not without some ethics. Loveless but not without some kindness. Hopeless but not without some redeeming qualities. The trick for Larissa had always been not pinning too much hope on the few traces of goodness she saw in them. For a long time she had lived with the hope that some day they might magically get better, stop stealing, start bathing, stop fighting, start loving. But when she had Owen she gave up on her nuclear family, choosing instead to start living correctly for herself and Owen. Her family would always be a part of her, but she wasn't dependent on them for her identity, security, or love anymore. Most of the time they simply exasperated her.

Work was always a relief. Not only was she able to concentrate on something besides her own family, but she was a contributing member of society, giving back to a community that had given her so much. Not that they had physically provided for her, but rather they had been willing to give her a chance, to see her as something other than another worthless Porter. She could see it in their eyes wherever she went, the recognition that she was something different, that she was the Porter who didn't steal, lie, or fight.

The day was shaping up to be slow so Larissa drove to the car repair shop—the only one in town—to check on her vehicle. The news was not good.

"We're not going to be able to fix it today," Bill Prince, the owner, informed her. "It's going to need a new transmission, and it's going to be about three thousand dollars. Sorry, Larissa, but you got as many miles from this as you're going to get without a complete overhaul. Because I like you, I'm going to tell you it would be better to buy a new car."

She sighed, thinking. A new car would be much more than three thousand and she hadn't finished paying for the one she already owned. In its current state, she couldn't dream of getting any money for a trade. "How much longer can it go if I get a new transmission?"

"It depends on your engine. It's not in good shape, and when it goes, you're looking at a few thousand more," Bill said. Larissa took comfort in his sympathetic tone. At least he was honest and trustworthy.

"I don't know what to do," she said honestly. "I still owe a few hundred dollars on this car."

"If you want my opinion, then I think you should donate this car to charity. You'll get a tax write-off that can help make up for what you owe. Get a new car. This one isn't worth the time and effort it would take to put in the new transmission."

"Okay," Larissa said, trying to sound like a competent adult instead of a scared kid. She knew nothing about cars. The reason she got in trouble in the first place was because she had listened to a smooth-talking salesman who assured her the car he sold her was the most reliable one on the lot. A week later it was in the shop, the first in a long series of repairs.

"I'll arrange for the donation if you want," Bill said. "They'll pick it up, tow it away, and send you a certificate in the mail for your taxes."

"That would be great, Bill," she said. "Thanks so much."

He smiled. "You're welcome, Larissa. I'm sorry this car has been such a lemon for you."

She nodded, smiling despite her fear and anxiety, and climbed back in her cruiser. Fall was fast approaching. With it came cold weather, rain, and falling leaves—not ideal bike weather, not to mention that she couldn't take Owen anywhere on her bike. She would have to get a new car ASAP, but she only had a few thousand dollars in her emergency savings fund. Was it better to drain the savings and take a smaller loan or leave the nest egg and take a larger loan? Over the years, she had learned a lot about finances through trial and error, but she was a long way from expert. And there was no one she could turn to for help. Her parents' financial strategy was to use all their expendable welfare income on the lottery and hope they hit it rich someday.

Even if she knew what to buy, how was she supposed to go car shopping with Owen in tow? Should she perch him on her handlebars and ride to Lexington? Yet there was no suitable sitter she trusted. In the end she decided to take a half day of personal time while Owen was in school. She liked to save her precious vacation days to spend with Owen, but this couldn't be helped.

Larissa fought an undertow of frustration. Her entire childhood had been out of her control. She swore when she was an adult that she would be in control of every situation, but she was fast learning that control was an illusion. Life happened. The only way to survive was to go with the flow and try to maintain a positive outlook. Buying a new car would make things tighter financially than she was comfortable with, but at least there was the possibility of buying something that was actually reliable. In the long run she might save money if she didn't have to take her car to the shop every month.

Her workday was mundane, providing her with too much time to dwell on her problems so that by the time she rode her bike to the Honeywell's farm, she was in a roaring bad mood. Like always, though, she attempted to stuff down her frustration in time to greet her son. It wasn't Owen's fault that she'd had a bad day.

She dismounted her bike midstride, the last few paces standing on one pedal working like a charm to lift her bad mood. But as soon as she came to a complete stop, her nerves woke up and began to jangle. She had only been to the farm once before, and that had been years ago. The feeling that she wasn't good enough to enter the pristine beauty still hadn't gone away. Owen was good enough, though, and he was here somewhere, waiting on her. That gave her the courage she needed to go forward and look for him.

She found him in one of the horse barns, standing on a chair beside Everett and still two feet shorter. The sight was heartrending for a number of reasons, mostly because she was seeing what her son most yearned for, but could never have, and his interaction with a father figure heaped all the more guilt on her head.

"Hey, buddy," she said, feigning cheerfulness.

Owen whirled to look at her while Everett took his time, turning slowly, but they both wore matching smiles. "Is it time to go already?" Owen said, disappointed.

"Yes, but you're coming back tomorrow," she reminded him.

"All right," he said, sounding reluctant. "Can I finish up this horse?"

"Sure," she said, standing back to watch. She had never seen any of the amazing barns before, had never seen Everett in action, and both were something to see. The barn was nicer than most houses, clean, architecturally interesting, and heated. "Did you design this barn?" she asked Everett. He was an architect, something she had always found odd since he mostly worked with horses.

"Nah, this was built when I was little. But eventually we'll expand again, and I intend to design those places."

She wondered why he became an architect. Was it the beauty of this building and his family's gothic style house that had inspired him? But asking him would lead them to a more personal relationship than she cared to have. As far as she was concerned, they were polite strangers and would remain that way forever, even if he was watching Owen for her.

"I think we're done," Everett said. "Good job today, Owen. Thanks for the help."

Owen beamed under his praise, squirming with delight as he jumped down from the chair. He ran over to Larissa and stopped short in front of her, belatedly realizing he didn't want to show affection in front of Everett. Larissa was having none of it, though. She stepped forward and hugged him, kissing the top of his head before he could squirm away.

"Love you," she whispered.

He wrinkled his nose, silently telling her she was pushing the affection thing too far. She smiled and ruffled his hair, letting him go.

"How's the transmission?" Everett asked as he led the horse back to its stall.

"Shot," Larissa said, trying not to reveal any of her anxiety. "Looks like we're getting a new car," she added, smiling at Owen.

"Really?" Owen asked, jumping up and down in his enthusiasm. "Can we get a convertible?"

Larissa laughed. "I don't think so, buddy. Put that on your wish list for when you're bigger."

Owen nodded. "Can it at least be red? Red cars are the best."

"We'll see," Larissa said. Having a color in mind was the most direction she had, and so she didn't say no. "What do you say to Mr. Honeywell?"

"Thank you," Owen said, dutifully turning in the direction Everett had gone.

"Anytime," Everett called.

"Thank you," Larissa added, impressed with her cool detachment. "Come on, bud." She rested her arm on Owen's shoulder and led him from the horse barn. Picking up her bike where she had left it, they began walking down the long lane and toward home.

"Hold up," Everett called, crunching gravel as he ran up beside them. "What are you doing?"

"Going home," Larissa said, confused.

"Larissa, you are not riding your bike all the way home."

"Of course not," Larissa patiently explained. "I can't ride it with Owen; we'll walk."

Everett didn't reply, he simply grabbed her bike and headed

toward his SUV. When he realized he wasn't being followed, though, he stopped and turned around. "Come on," he said.

Larissa gritted her teeth at his imperious tone. Why oh why couldn't she face these situations when she was alone and could actually argue about them? To argue in front of Owen might undo all the politeness and good manners she had tried to instill in him. "Thank you for the ride," she said through gritted teeth as they stalked toward the sleek SUV.

"Ow, Mom, you're hurting my neck," Owen said, shaking free of her tight clutch.

"Sorry, honey," Larissa said, taking a deep breath and aiming for calm. Beside them, Everett chuckled softly.

"Everett, can you stay for supper?" Owen said.

"Owen," Larissa snapped, then, remembering her manners again. "I'm sure Mr. Honeywell has better things to do with his evening."

"No, Mr. Honeywell doesn't. Supper sounds nice, if it's okay with you." He darted her a look and a smile.

"We'd love to have you," Larissa lied, unable to feign a smile or convincing tone. In response, he chuckled again.

CHAPTER 5

"*Larissa is a nerd!*"

The taunting probably wouldn't have hurt her feelings except that it was coming from her brother. And not any brother, but Nick, her closest brother in age. For some reason he seemed to take Larissa's good grades personally.

"So? Mrs. Friend says nerds grow up to make the most money," Larissa returned. They were standing outside the grocery store, waiting on their mother to empty her pockets of all her expendable cash on cigarettes and beer for her weekly Friday night end-of-work celebration. Larissa wondered if her father would be joining the festivities this week or if he would arrive home too late, triggering a fight because her mother would have already used up all their supplies by herself. Which was worse, to have both her parents drunk and yelling at their children, or to have one of them drunk and yelling at each other?

"Yeah, well you don't have any friends," Nick yelled.

"Neither do you," she returned. She had no idea what had her brother so angry tonight. What had set him off? It wasn't even report card day.

"You take that back. I got friends."

"It's I have, Nick, and no you don't," she said. She didn't usually correct

his grammar, knowing it would infuriate him, but he was so mean sometimes. Lately it seemed like he picked on her all the time.

"Shut up, Larissa," Nick said, clapping her upside the head with his palm. At the physical contact, something within Larissa broke. Maybe it was ten years of repressed anger finally finding a target. Whatever the reason, she leapt on her brother, knocking him to the ground. They were both small for their age, but Nick was especially tiny. Even though he was almost two years older, he and Larissa were about the same size. He tried to fight her off, but it was useless. She hit him again and again, whaling any part of him she could reach with her small fists, screaming and crying in rage.

"Leave me alone," she repeated over and over. "Leave me alone. I hate you; I hate all of you."

Somehow she wasn't surprised when the strong arm clamped around her waist, dragging her off her brother. Everett Honeywell seemed to posses a sixth sense about when she needed him. Or maybe she was creating such a ruckus that the whole town knew about it.

"I'm telling Mom," Nick said, jumping to his feet with the resilience of someone who was used to receiving a beating. "And then you're going to get your butt whipped." He ran off into the store to find their mother.

Larissa dangled helplessly in Everett's arm, her toes a good foot off the pavement. Nick's threat caused her no fear. What she feared more was Everett's disappointed reaction.

"Okay?" he asked.

She nodded, feeling miserable.

"What happened?" he asked, his tone gentle as he set her down and turned her to face him.

"He called me names. He was picking on me." Again, she added mentally, sniffling.

"Did he throw the first punch, or did you?" Everett asked.

"He hit me in the side of the head, but I jumped on him and knocked him down."

Everett gave her a half smile. "Let's sit down," he suggested. They sat on the curb, reminding Larissa of their last conversation at this very market two years before. "Lissy, there's a difference in defending yourself and attacking someone. Especially when you're the stronger one."

"He did hit me, Everett, and we're the same size," Larissa defended.

"I know, but I wasn't talking about physical strength. You're stronger in here." He tapped his heart. "You're intelligent, polite, and well behaved. Your brother isn't any of those things."

"Don't I know it," Larissa said ruefully.

"My point is that you're better off than Nick is, probably better off than he'll ever be unless he makes some drastic changes. It's up to you to be the bigger person and walk away. Don't lower yourself to his level. Understand?"

"I think so," she said. "But what am I supposed to do if he hits me?"

"Tell your parents."

She looked at him in confusion, not sure how that was supposed to help. "They yell at me for being too stupid to move out of his way."

Everett sighed, the same longsuffering sigh he used whenever her family was mentioned. "Then tell me. If things get bad then Nick and I will have a little talk."

"I don't think that will go over well."

"Of course it won't," he said. "That's the whole point, but he'll be sure and leave you alone if he knows someone as big as me is on your side. Guys like Nick, they look for weakness. By refusing to fight with him, you're showing him you're stronger. But if that doesn't work, then we'll use a language he understands and I'll have a word with him."

"Okay," Larissa said, sounding significantly more cheerful. She was beginning to recognize a certain feeling when she was with Everett. If she had to put a name to it, then she would call it security. She felt safe when she was with him, like nothing in the world could hurt her or go wrong. "Did you get your driver's license yet?"

He wagged his eyebrows and reached for his wallet, withdrawing official identification with his name on it.

Larissa took it, studying his picture. She whistled appreciatively. "Wow, Everett, you're like a real grownup now."

He laughed. "Sixteen's not so old, Lissy."

"It's old enough to have a baby. My sister had a baby when she was sixteen, and so did my brother's girlfriend."

His smile was replaced by a frown as he reached for his license. "That's not going to happen to me."

"No, probably not," she said, vaguely understanding that his family didn't do anything like her family. After all, he had three older brothers, and none of them had babies yet.

"And you're not going to go that route either, are you, Lissy?" he pressed, his tone suddenly serious.

She wrinkled her nose and shook her head violently back and forth. "No way. I hate boys. I'm never letting one stick his tongue down my throat to make a baby."

Everett laughed a long time over that comment.

"What's funny?" she asked.

"Nothing," he said. "Keep thinking that way for as long as possible."

"I will. I don't like boys." She frowned. "I don't like girls, either. I don't really have any friends."

"You have me," he said.

"Yeah, I guess I do," she said, feeling suddenly shy.

"I don't have any friends outside of my brothers. Except you."

"Am I really your friend, Everett?" Larissa asked, peeking at him from under her lashes.

"Sure you are. You and I, we're simpatico."

"What's that mean?" she asked.

"Look it up," he said. With a smile, he stood and ruffled her hair before he walked away. Larissa watched him until he was out of sight, and then she sat staring at the place where he had been, wondering if he was somehow magic.

CHAPTER 6

"We're having fish," Larissa blurted nervously as soon as they stepped inside her tiny house. "It has a lot of omega 3's, and an article I read said that's healthy for brain development in children. It's the low mercury kind of fish." She paused, licking her lips and darting her eyes around the living room. "I could make you something else if you want." *Or you could go away and leave us in peace.*

"Fish is fine," Everett said. "I'm not a picky eater."

"That's good," Larissa babbled, nodding approvingly. "I try to teach Owen the importance of eating whatever is set before him. He's sort of hit or miss, though. He'll eat it eventually, but not without a whole lot of complaining."

Everett was smiling mildly as he listened to her flow of words.

"I'll get started on supper. It shouldn't take too long."

"Take your time; it's not even five yet."

"We eat early because Owen goes to bed at eight," Larissa needlessly explained.

"That's a reasonable bedtime."

They stopped speaking then, staring at each other. Down the hall, Owen was using the bathroom and washing his hands, the splashing sound alerting her to the fact that the sink was on full blast and probably overflowing, but she couldn't muster a word of direction to her son. Instead, she stared at Everett, dry mouthed as he stared at her.

"Liss," he whispered, taking a step forward. That broke Larissa from her trance. She turned and fled toward the kitchen.

"I won't be too long," she yelled, but there was no need to yell; he was on her heels.

"Can I help?" he offered.

She sighed, relieved that he wasn't pursuing whatever he had been about to pursue when he whispered her name. "Sure, you can help Owen set the table. He'll show you where everything is when he gets here. Owen!" she called, hurrying him along.

"What, Mom? I'm right here," Owen said.

"Can you please show Mr. Honeywell where the plates are? He's going to help you set the table."

"Okay," Owen said, straightening his shoulders as if he had been handed an assignment of vital importance. He then proceeded not only to point out the plates, but to explain how to set a formal table, much to Larissa's delight. *He does listen to me sometimes,* she thought, smiling as she set out the fish and seasoned it. She put rice in the microwave and cut up a fruit salad as the two men moved their topic to football. Everett was much more knowledgeable about the sport than she. He and Owen were having such a detailed discussion that she was surprised how deeply Owen grasped the sport. Maybe an intricate knowledge of sports was built into the Y-chromosome.

Due to the quick-cooking nature of fish, supper was ready in twenty minutes, which was a relief to Larissa. The sooner she got this evening over, the sooner she could breathe easier again. Of course she should have known things never work out like she hoped they might.

"I thought after supper we might go car shopping," Everett said.

"Can we, Mom? Can we, please, please, please?"

"I don't think that's a good idea," Larissa said

"Why not?" Owen asked.

Larissa couldn't think of one excuse other than "because I said so," and she certainly couldn't employ that one with Everett sitting nearby, hanging on every word. "It's a school night," she said at last.

"We could be back in plenty of time for bed if that's what you're worried about," Everett said, causing Owen to squirm in his chair and dart his mother anxious looks. "C'mon, Lissy," he added when he sensed she was wavering. "When else are you going to go? I'm offering you a ride and my vast knowledge of cars."

He had her there, drat him and his superior knowledge. "All right," she said. "Thank you."

"It's not getting any easier to say those words to me, is it?" Everett asked.

Owen looked back and forth between them. "Why would it be hard for her to say? She makes me say 'thank you' all the time."

"Everett is teasing me, honey," Larissa explained.

"Why?" Owen asked.

"Because she's pretty and that's what guys do—they tease pretty girls."

Owen looked at his plate as he thought that over. "There's a girl at school I like. Should I tease her?"

"Yes," Everett said at the same time Larissa said, "No."

"Everett," Larissa added, tossing him a disapproving look. "I don't want him teasing girls."

"It's what guys do, Liss. It's part of our DNA. Just make sure you're not mean," he added to Owen. "And don't hit her."

"I'm not allowed to hit girls," Owen said solemnly.

"See, he knows the rules," Everett said.

Larissa bit back her reply, wondering how long she would be able to do so. At one point would she simply explode, telling Everett to butt out of their lives? She hoped not because the sad fact was that she needed him, at least where Owen was concerned. Going to the Honeywell farm was a much better proposition than staying home alone every afternoon, something Larissa had hated since school started a few weeks ago.

She remained silent throughout dinner, though she could hardly get a word in edgewise with Owen quizzing Everett over every facet of horses and cars. It was as if he had been storing up thousands of questions to ask a man whenever he got the chance. They carried their plates into the kitchen together. Everett helped with the dishes while Owen sat on the counter and continued his inquisition. Larissa should probably intervene and tell him to stop, but she didn't want to crush his enthusiasm, and Everett didn't seem to mind.

When the dishes were finished, Larissa took out her favorite bottle of disinfectant to wipe down the counters and the table before giving the floor a quick once over with the broom. She didn't think anything of it until she realized Everett was watching her.

"You do that every day?" he asked.

"Yes," she said, her tone wary. "Why?"

"It's so clean in here the light bounces off the counter. Almost hurts my eyes." He smiled. She didn't.

"Mom likes to clean," Owen volunteered. "That's her favorite thing to do."

Larissa turned to the cupboard and stowed the broom so she wouldn't have to suffer under Everett's scrutiny any longer. It didn't take a professional psychologist to put two and two together and realize why she was obsessive about cleaning.

"She's very good at it," Everett said.

She turned in time to see Owen studying her and laughed. Hearing that his mother was pretty and good at something was almost too much for his little brain to take in. To him, she was merely Mom.

"I guess," he said at last. "But sometimes she does it too much."

"There's no such thing as too clean," Larissa said.

"She says that a lot, too," Owen added.

Larissa lifted him from the counter, nudging him toward the door. She wasn't at all certain how she felt about this sudden turn of events where she was the outsider and her son and Everett were co-conspirators together. For the last seven years, it had only been her and Owen. How did he so easily accept someone else into their lives?

Everett opened the car door for them and Owen scrambled inside, inserting himself in the middle. Larissa put her hand on the door to climb inside, but Everett placed his hands on her waist, easily lifting her up. Larissa's placid expression didn't change—she hoped—but inside everything shifted. It had been seven years since anyone but her son touched her, seven years since Everett touched her, but the feeling was the same one she had that long ago night when she was sixteen. Memories came crashing violently back, memories she had tried to repress: Everett's arms around her, his lips on hers. But along with the memories came resentment. Why did he have to show up now to disrupt her happy life? Maybe *happy* was too strong a word; maybe settled was a better description. She and Owen were settled. They were stable. After the chaos of her early years, she wanted nothing more than what she had now, and she certainly wasn't going to get all twitterpated and disrupt Owen's stability.

She took a deep breath, willing herself to calm down. Everett hadn't meant anything by politely giving her a lift. She was reading too much in to the simple touch. Things weren't going to change. He was being a friend and providing help, like he had done when she was a kid. Only she wasn't a kid anymore, and her reaction to him wasn't childlike. She squeezed her eyes shut and turned toward her window. This day was quickly become a nightmare. She needed to get some distance from Everett, the sooner, the better.

"You're quiet over there, Liss," Everett said, darting her a look from the corner of his eye. "Thinking about what kind of car you want?"

She turned to look at him then, struck anew by how handsome he was. It had taken her a long time to come to that realization. For most of her life, he had simply been Everett, her guardian angel. It wasn't until much later that she saw him a man, and that realization had sent her life into a tailspin. Even though she didn't want to think of him that way now, she was helpless to stop; he was incredibly nice looking with his thick black hair, black eyes, and dark lashes. All of the brothers looked alike, and all of them were devilishly handsome.

"No, I wasn't thinking of the car," she answered at last. "I'm afraid I know next to nothing about cars."

"What do you want in a car?"

"Reliability, safety, and good gas mileage," she answered automatically with the three things her last car had lacked.

"That's doable. Is it okay if I do the talking?"

She laughed. "Uh, yes, I think that's okay," she said mildly, thinking it was a dream come true. Salesmen tended to look at her youthful features and see a walking target. "I don't have much to spend," she hastened to add, biting her lip. "And I probably won't be able to get a good loan rate. One of my brothers stole my identity to open a few credit cards."

He sighed. "Of course they did," he muttered. "Did you prosecute?"

She shook her head. "I wanted the mess to go away, and it's not like he would have learned anything from the punishment. And he has a half dozen kids to support." She smiled, forcing the unpleasant topic away. "You have nieces now, don't you?"

He nodded, smiling. "Three and one on the way. Genevieve looks ready to pop, though that could be because she's only thigh high."

Larissa had glimpsed Darcy's wife a few times, and she was as tiny as Everett said. Together, she and Darcy were an ill fit, but they seemed very happy together. "Is she doing okay?" The whole town kept up with the Honeywells, their local celebrities, and therefore everyone knew of Genevieve's double brush with leukemia.

"Everything looks good," Everett said. "They've been in town the last few days, but they're heading back to their farm tomorrow."

Larissa marveled at the sadness in his tone. He was actually going to miss his brother and sister-in-law. The only thing she had ever felt when one of her siblings went away was relief. She chuckled. "Our lives couldn't be more opposite, you know that?"

"And yet we're very much the same," Everett said, taking his eyes off the road to give her a warm smile that robbed her of her amusement and left her breathless.

"Why are you the same?" Owen said, looking between them for similarities.

"Well, we're both middle children in big families," Everett said. "And we're both quiet. We both like to learn new things. We both think character is important—that's what's inside a person. We both grew up in this town. And we're friends. Don't you think that's a lot of things we have in common?"

"Do you like to clean, too? Cause that's Mom's favorite."

"Owen," Larissa said, her embarrassment growing when Everett chuckled.

"Probably not as much as your mom does," Everett said, winking at Larissa over the top of her son's head.

"She also likes to take showers a lot. I asked my friends, but none of their moms take more than one shower a day like she does."

Larissa put her hand over his mouth. "That's enough, Owen. Everett doesn't need to hear any more of my hobbies, okay?"

Owen nodded and she removed her hand. She was sure her cheeks were three shades of red. Not only was it embarrassing for him to blurt to Everett that she liked to take showers, but he had told other kids at school. "Merciful heavens," she muttered, turning to look out her window.

Everett's chuckle deepened to outright laughter and after a few seconds Larissa joined him so that by the time they pulled up in front of the car dealership, they were laughing loudly with Owen looking curiously back and forth between them.

"What?" he asked. "What's funny?"

"Nothing," Larissa said, swiping at her eyes. "Please don't tell the car dealer anything about me, okay?"

"Okay," he said, affronted at the thought that they might be laughing at him.

Larissa patted his leg reassuringly, and his mood lightened, though she thought it was probably due to the fact that he glimpsed the rows upon rows of shiny cars. "Awesome," he breathed, looking at a red convertible a few rows down. Larissa tamped down her instinct to remind him such a car was impractical, not wanting to be a dream squisher.

"Is that the kind of car you're going to put on your wish list?" she asked instead.

He nodded, his eyes never leaving the car.

"You'll look great in it," she said, giving his knee a squeeze.

He smiled and she turned to see Everett standing beside the car, waiting to help her down. His look was intent, but she had no idea what it meant, only that it made her heart thud painfully in response. She placed her hand in his and hopped down. He squeezed her hand and might have kept it if not for the solicitous salesman who tripped all over himself trying to get to them. Larissa had the mental image of the sales staff having a fistfight in their eagerness to try and get to a Honeywell.

"What can I do for you today, Mr. Honeywell?"

Was it her imagination, or did the salesman wipe a trail of drool from his chin?

"Actually, this lady is your customer today. She's a close friend of mine."

"Yes, of course," the salesman said, genuflecting his neck like a bobble-head doll. "We'll treat her like family." He smiled, showing all of his teeth. "What can I help you with, Miss…?"

"Porter," Larissa supplied, and then she saw it—the salesman's instantaneous reaction to her name as he did a mental recalculation of what a Honeywell could afford verses what a Porter could afford. "I'm not actually sure what I'm looking for. Everett had some ideas, I think." She turned questioning, hopeful eyes to Everett who once again took over the conversation.

"Here's what we're looking for," Everett said, beginning a long string of conversation Larissa couldn't comprehend. The salesman must have, though, because he nodded his head a few times and led them to a car.

The first thing that jumped out at Larissa was the price. It would be a stretch, but it was doable. The second thing was the color.

"It's blue," Owen said, sounding disappointed. Larissa laid a restraining hand on his shoulder.

"It's very pretty," she said. "Do you by chance have it in red?"

"I do, but it's a newer model and more expensive," the salesman warned.

"Let's see it," Everett said.

Owen gasped at his first sight of the car. "Mom, it's awesome," he exclaimed. "It's perfect!"

Indeed, it did look perfect. It also looked like much more car than

Larissa could afford. The sticker on the window was confirmation of her fear.

"This is beautiful," she said regretfully. "But it's too much."

The salesman nodded as if he'd expected as much, but Everett was undeterred. "We'll take this car for that price," he said, pointing to the first car they'd been shown.

"Now, Mr. Honeywell, you know I'm willing to work with you, but that's a mighty big leap."

"I also know what the book value is on this car, and I know you'll still be clearing a margin of about fifteen hundred," Everett said. He sounded and looked so confident. Larissa hadn't managed to overcome her timidity unless it was on the job. There she was confident and in charge, but she was paid to be. Away from work she was a clueless twenty-three year old.

"I don't know," the salesman replied, swiping his hand over his chin.

"Give us the price, and we'll pay cash today," Everett offered.

"Deal," the man agreed, his eyes gleaming. Larissa started to protest, but Everett clasped her hand, giving it a squeeze. "I'll go draw up the papers." The man turned and sprinted toward the dealership, practically rubbing his hands together in glee.

"Everett," Larissa hissed, snatching her hand from him clutch. "I can't pay cash for this. That's much more than I have in savings."

"Obviously I meant I was going to pay for it. You can pay me back."

She was momentarily stunned speechless by the fact that he had ten thousand dollars lying around in his checking account, and then she realized he probably had at least ten times that amount and then some.

"No, absolutely not," Larissa said. Grabbing Owen's hand, she pivoted toward Everett's SUV. He caught up with her in two steps, resting his hand on her shoulder.

"Lissy, this is how business is done; you pay cash, you get a better deal. Everyone knows that."

Larissa hadn't, but then she could never imagine having enough cash to pay for a vehicle outright. "Yes, that's a good idea when you're buying your own car. But you can't go around buying cars for people."

"Why not? I have the money for it, and you need a car."

"Because…because…" she cast about, aiming for a reasonable explanation. "Because you're losing interest on your money, that's why."

"So pay me the interest I'm losing from my bank. It'll still be lower than the interest you'll pay on a car loan, especially with your credit rating."

She put a hand to her head and puffed a sigh of exasperation, hating how he made everything sound so reasonable when, really, it wasn't reasonable at all. She wanted to put her foot down and outright refuse his offer. But logic told her that she desperately needed a car. Everett's offer assured that she would pay thousands less than if she did it on her own. If she gave in, though, she would be beholden to him. Again. How could she stand it?

With a glance at Owen, she swallowed her pride. Taking care of her son was more important than her pride; those few thousand dollars could mean the difference between survival and going under for her family. "All right, Everett. But we're going to set up a payment schedule and sign a contract."

"I wouldn't have it any other way," Everett replied, but by his teasing tone she knew he didn't mean a word of it. He rested his hand on the small of her back, steering her toward the dealership. They parked by her car and she felt a thrill, though she didn't know if it was caused by the car or Everett's hand on her back.

"It's so pretty," Larissa whispered.

"Then it fits you," Everett said as softly. She bit her lip, hiding her smile as he led her inside.

arissa looked pretty, or so she thought. Her sister, Shelby, had other ideas.

"Can't you walk straight?" she asked, turning to scowl at Larissa.

"I've never walked in heels before," Larissa said for at least the dozenth time that day.

Shelby rolled her eyes. "At least stop slouching. And don't cross your arms over your chest. I didn't stuff your bra so you could cover it up. Here, let me put on another layer of lipstick. Smile. Not like that, stupid, like this." She demonstrated by jutting her bottom lip and tipping her lips in a barely perceptible smile.

Larissa tried hard to mimic her, feeling ridiculous.

Shelby studied her little sister with a sneer of disgust. "Good enough, I suppose. Now remember, if anyone asks, you're fourteen."

"But I'm twelve," Larissa said, earning another eye roll from Shelby.

"I know, stupid, but for tonight you're fourteen. Geez, I'm going to kill Kelsey for canceling on me tonight and making me drag you along." She turned and began walking before stopping to glare at her sister again. "And don't mention anything about the British president."

"Prime Minister," Larissa corrected.

"I don't care, Larissa. No one cares. Shut up about it. In fact, don't say anything at all."

Larissa nodded, biting her lip before remembering it was coated in lipstick. "What if he wants to kiss me?"

"Then kiss him," Shelby said, the disgust in her tone conveying that the question should have been self-explanatory. "Do whatever it takes to make him happy. Got it?"

"O-okay," Larissa stammered. Surely her sister didn't really mean that, did she? But as she watched Shelby's practiced saunter, she realized she probably did.

I might kiss him if he's nice, but I won't do more than that, Larissa promised herself. She was vaguely curious about kissing since she was seemingly the last girl in the seventh grade who hadn't kissed a boy. But, as such, she also knew what happened after kissing, and she wanted no part of that.

"There they are," Shelby said, sending Larissa's heartbeat into overdrive. *Would he be cute? Would he be nice? Would he like her?*

"Here we are, guys," Shelby announced, plopping down in her date's lap before sliding across him with a smile. There was no way Larissa was doing that. She stood nervously at the end of the table, her hands clasped behind her back. Her date looked up and he was cute, she supposed. She had only recently begun thinking about boys, and she hadn't decided what made a male desirable or not.

"Where's Kelsey?" the boy asked.

"She couldn't make it. This is my sister, Larissa. She's fourteen," Shelby said, glaring defiantly at Larissa lest she intercede with the truth.

Larissa didn't say a word, though; she was too nervous.

"Fourteen's a little young, but she's cute," the guy said, patting the seat beside him. Tentatively, Larissa sat down. "I'm Tim. Why haven't I seen you around school?"

"Oh, um, you know," Larissa said, twisting her fingers in her lap. She darted a helpless look at Shelby. She had never been good at lying. Shelby, on the other hand, was fluent.

"Larissa's smart. She hangs with the advanced kids," Shelby explained.

"A smart Porter. Wow." Tim grinned at Larissa who smiled tentatively in return. "Say something intelligent," he urged.

"World beef prices are tumbling due to Mad Cow Disease," she said, making it sound like a question. Was that an intelligent thing to say, or plain weird?

Tim laughed. "Wow, you are smart. I've never even heard of Mad Cow Disease."

"You will. People are dying. It's about to become world news."

Under the table, Shelby kicked her.

Larissa cleared her throat. "So tell me about you." That was one piece of Shelby's advice that had seemed logical; when in doubt, ask him about himself. According to Shelby, men loved to talk about themselves. And it appeared to be true. Tim began a long discourse on his interests, namely his band. Coincidentally, Larissa was a big fan of music, and they made an immediate connection bonding over mutually favorite songs.

"I love Britney Spears," Shelby inserted.

"You would," Tim said. "Your sister has much better taste." He turned to wink at Larissa, smiling. She returned his smile with more confidence this time. This wasn't so hard. All she had to do was be herself. The evening was shaping up to be a good one, not least of which because Shelby had told her the guys were paying for dinner, meaning she could get a full meal for once. She turned her attention to the menu when she felt it, Tim's hand riding high on her leg, pushing up her skirt. Instinctively, she shoved it away, causing Tim to laugh.

"You really aren't like your sister," he said. "Okay, we'll slow it down a little." He removed his hand, settling his arm on the back of the booth instead. Since he wasn't touching her, Larissa relaxed, studying her menu again.

"The Honeywells are here," Shelby's date said. "Wonder how long it will take for them to get thrown out this time?" He, Tim, and Shelby snickered. Larissa didn't join in. Instead, she dropped her menu on the table and looked frantically around the restaurant until she spotted them—all five of them— seated in a far booth, talking and laughing among themselves. Everett leaned back, smiling, at least until he caught Larissa in his peripheral vision. Then he did a double take, glowering at her across the room.

"Whoa, what's that about?" Shelby's date asked.

"I think he's jealous," Shelby said. "He's always had a thing for me."

"Which one is it? I can't ever tell them apart," Tim said.

"Neither can I, but it doesn't matter; they all like me," Shelby said.

"You wish," her date said, shoving lightly at her arm.

"They don't like anyone local," Tim said. "Town girls aren't good enough for their royal highnesses. And forget about ever dating Ivy. I tried to ask her out once and one of them stuffed me in a locker."

"Maybe it was that one. Maybe that's why he's glaring at you," Shelby's date suggested.

"I don't think it was him. He's the tallest, I would have remembered that. I think it was one of the shorter ones. Who knows? They're a bunch of rich snobs anyway."

"No they're not," Larissa said. "They're really nice, and they do a lot for the community. They paid for fireworks last year, and they have scholarships and all kinds of other stuff. Our town would probably die without them."

The other three people at her table looked at her as if she had sprouted horns and wings. "Okay," Shelby's date drawled. "Someone's been drinking the kool-aid."

"We don't have any kool-aid," Shelby said, confused.

"He's not talking about actual kool-aid," Larissa explained. "It's a cult reference. You know, Jim Jones."

Shelby glared at her and shook her head, but Tim laughed. "You're a trip, Larissa. You're like the cutest little encyclopedia ever." He removed his arm from the booth, resting it on her shoulder to give her a squeeze.

She smiled, pleased at the compliment. It was sort of disconcerting to her that her sister had been right all along; dating was fun.

Their laughter continued over supper, though the three older teens talked about things and people that meant nothing to Larissa. Sometimes the things they said made her uncomfortable, though it wasn't so much what they said as how they said it. There was something in their tone that let her know there was more going on than what she realized. Sometimes she saw a certain look exchanged between Tim and Shelby's date. She didn't know what it meant, but it made her uneasy.

He was being nice to her, though, and he did pay for dinner, which she thought was generous. If I can get a date every weekend, I might actually eat enough to put some weight on, she thought. Maybe that was why Shelby liked to go out so often—for the food.

"The big Honeywell is still looking at us," Shelby's date said. "He's giving me the creeps. You guys ready to go?"

"I'm ready," Shelby said, her sultry tone spiking Larissa's discomfort again, especially when her date laughed and leaned in to pinch her under the table.

"You're always ready," he said.

"Are you ready, Larissa?" Tim asked, his tone matching that of Shelby's date.

"I guess so," she said uncertainly. If he was asking if she was ready to leave, then the answer was yes because all her food was gone. She wasn't sure that was what he meant, though she had no idea what else it might be.

He laughed. "Ready as you'll ever be, huh?"

"Uh huh," she said, thoroughly confused. She slid out of the booth, waiting for him to slide out. She darted one more glance at Everett who was glaring at their group. She had no idea why he should be angry with her; she wasn't doing anything wrong. Was she?

They walked to the parking lot, and there they started to diverge. "Aren't you riding with us?" she asked Shelby, sounding as nervous as she felt.

Shelby turned to give her a derisive laugh. "No, stupid. Why would we ride with you? I'll see you later at home." With that, she turned and followed her date to his car.

"But..." Larissa called, feeling helpless. She should have guessed that Shelby would dump her at the first available opportunity, but it still surprised her that her sister would have so little care for her wellbeing as to leave her with a total stranger. She looked up at Tim, her eyes wide. He smiled and clasped her hand.

"C'mon, little Larissa. Don't look so petrified."

But I am petrified, she thought, trotting behind him, barely able to keep upright in her too-high heels. He didn't open the door for her, he simply let her go while he opened his own door, waiting for her to find her way to the passenger side. She did, closing the door with a bang that made her jump.

"Where are we going?" she asked, once again twining her hands in her lap.

"My place. My parents are out for the night. We could watch a movie."

"Okay," she said, relaxing slightly. She could handle a movie; she liked movies.

He turned to smile at her. "You're a pretty little thing. I can't believe I never noticed you before with your long hair and big, brown eyes. Brown eyes are my favorite."

"They are?" she whispered. Her dinner lodged in her throat, making her feel like she might throw up.

He nodded. "Is this your first date?"

Now it was her turn to nod.

"What about kissing? Do any of those braniacs you hang out with know how to kiss?"

"Not to my knowledge," she said.

He chuckled, shifting in his seat so he was facing her. "Then it's good you came to me; it's my best subject by far." His arm slid around her waist while his other hand settled uncomfortably high on her thigh. She shied away from him, shrinking into the seat when he advanced, and then suddenly he wasn't there anymore. Instead, he was dangling in midair outside the car.

"She's twelve," Everett said, the words piercing the sudden silence like daggers.

"I didn't know, man, I swear," Tim said, his voice shaking. "Shelby told me she was fourteen."

"And fourteen is old enough for what you had planned? I don't think so."

"Look, no harm, no foul. I didn't touch her, you can ask her." He darted a frantic look at Larissa, hoping she would back up his story.

"That's good," Everett said. "And now you're going to go tell all of your friends and even the people you don't like that if anyone so much as looks at her again, I will hold you personally responsible. I will find you, and I will turn you inside out. Are we clear?"

Tim nodded, terrified beyond speech. Everett let him go and he sagged helplessly against the car.

"Let's go, Larissa," Everett commanded, ripping open her door with such force that it was in danger of popping off its hinges.

Larissa hopped out, trotting along behind him, her heels clacking on the asphalt. He opened the passenger door to his car, waiting until she was safely tucked inside before slamming it, then he slid behind the wheel and sat there, gripping it until his knuckles became white.

"I'm sorry, Everett," Larissa whispered. She had no idea what she had done wrong, but something had made him furious.

"I'm not mad at you," Everett said, easing his grip on the steering wheel. "I'm mad thinking about what might have happened to you if I hadn't been here."

Larissa shuddered. Though she had only a vague awareness of what he was referring to, she was still properly terrified. "It was fun up until the car."

"You can't go out with guys like that," Everett said patiently.

"Guys like what?"

"Guys who only want one thing."

"But he seemed so nice. And he bought me supper."

"Liss, I'm going to tell you a secret about guys. They'll do whatever it takes to get what they want. They'll buy you dinner or say pretty words, anything, until you're putty in their hands. And you're too young for any of that."

"How old is old enough?"

He finally turned to look at her, smiling. "For you? Twenty five."

Larissa laughed. "No, really, Everett. How will I know when I'm ready to date?"

"You'll know. In the mean time, don't let anyone pressure you into it if you're not ready. Not your sister, not a guy. Not anyone."

"Okay," she said, feeling oddly relieved. "Sometimes I still play with dolls," she said, confessing as if it was a great secret, which it was.

Everett nodded approvingly. "That's good, Lissy. You're a little girl; you should act like it. There's nothing wrong with that."

"Shelby says I'm too old for such stuff. She says it's time I turned my attention to boys."

"Shelby's wrong," Everett said vehemently.

"You know Shelby?" she asked. They weren't in the same grade.

"Everyone knows Shelby," he said, using the resigned tone he seemed to reserve when talking about her family. "Don't take this the wrong way, but I don't want you to turn out like your sister. You're meant for bigger things. You're going to go to college and have a career."

Larissa nodded. She could believe it when he said it. On her own, her future seemed like a hopeless pipe dream. He started the car and they drove to her trailer park in silence. When he parked, she put her hand on the door, but he held her back.

"I'm leaving for college next week," he said.

The announcement hit Larissa like a fist to the gut. What would she do without her protector, her guardian angel, her friend? "Oh," she said, sitting back against the seat with a thump.

He fished in his pocket and handed her a slip of paper. "Here's my number. If you ever need anything, you can call. And if you get in real trouble, call one of my brothers. Any of them will help you."

She nodded, knowing she would never call any of his brothers, and probably never call him. Their worlds were separate, only occasionally intersecting when she needed him. Otherwise, they didn't communicate with each other. She stared at the number, unable to read it in the dim moonlight.

"Maybe you'll find a girlfriend and get married," she said, the thought making her somehow sad. Why, though? She only wanted the best for him, and a pretty, perfect wife was definitely for the best.

He chuckled. "I don't think so," he said.

"Why not?"

"I'm not interested in getting involved with anyone. I like my life exactly as it is. Women make demands; they change you. I don't want to change."

Larissa nodded. "That makes sense," she said. "I don't want to change for a man, either."

"See? Great minds think alike."

She smiled. "Everett, what do you think of the Prime Minister of Britain?"

"I think he's a great man who's shaping up to be one of our strongest allies. I was glad when he got elected. What do you think?"

"The same," she replied. They shared a smile. "I should go," she said, reaching for the door again. She opened it and was half out before she turned to duck her head back inside. "I'll miss you," she said, the half-whispered words coming out in a rush.

"I'll miss you too, Lissy," he said, as softly and quickly.

CHAPTER 8

$\mathcal{I}$f Larissa thought Everett would go home after she secured
her car, she was mistaken.

"Thank you," she said, sincerely this time and without having to
force the words. "You have no idea how much this evening has
helped us."

In reply, Everett smiled. "I'll make sure you get home okay."

"Oh, all right," she replied, surprised. "You really don't have to.
We'll be fine." Owen was already having longer and longer blinks,
telling her that a meltdown was on the way if she didn't get him to
bed soon.

"I insist," Everett said in the tone he had used when she was a child,
the one that told her he was in charge and arguing was pointless.

"Suit yourself," she said, some of her gratitude wearing away.
Driving her new car renewed some of her good humor. Belatedly she
realized she probably should have taken a test drive to make sure she
liked the car. The fact that she hadn't either showed her great faith in
Everett or her great ignorance of the process. Either way, she loved
the car. It was comfortable, and it actually purred—unlike her last car
which had coughed and chugged so loudly that people always turned
to look wherever she showed up.

"We're home," Larissa announced, stating the obvious when Everett followed them inside.

"So I see," he said. "I was hoping to have a word with you." He didn't add *alone,* but he did glance significantly toward Owen.

"I have to give Owen a bath and put him to bed," Larissa said.

"I'll wait on the couch if that's okay."

"Okay," she said, feeling unaccountably nervous. What could he possibly want to talk to her about? Maybe it was about the car repayment schedule. That was certainly something she wanted to talk to him about. Though she knew it wasn't likely, she soothed her jangled nerves by believing he was actually waiting on her couch to talk business.

Owen was a little boy who liked his schedule. Since it was already a half hour past his bedtime, he was in rare form, dragging his feet on the way to his bath and then having a meltdown tantrum when he couldn't find his favorite toy. Larissa did her best to ignore him and hurry him along, embarrassed that Everett was privy to such a display. He was down the hall in the living room, but Owen's tantrum was probably loud enough for the neighbors to hear.

At last she tucked her son into bed with a kiss, noting that he was fast asleep by the time she left the room. He was only an hour past his normal bedtime, but she knew there might be retribution the next day. Owen didn't cope well when he was off schedule. She smiled, remembering the nights during her childhood when she had stayed awake till the wee hours of the morning watching television or listening to her parents fight. Sometimes it was because the cops had been called and the whole house was in an uproar. On those days, she had mostly slept through school, but her teachers were always kind and understanding. Looking back, Larissa wondered if they knew what her home life was like and offered her extra care and support because of it. Whatever the reason, they had been very patient with her, and it had made a difference. Despite being so tired she could barely function on some days, she had excelled in school.

When she returned to her family room, Everett was watching a baseball game. She paused in the entryway, taking in the sight of him sprawled on her couch. He was so large that he made the sofa look like a miniature, his legs sticking up awkwardly like a daddy-long-leg spider. He couldn't have been very comfortable, but he looked right somehow, as if he had been there all along.

Sensing her approach, he turned to her with a welcoming smile. He turned off the television and placed the remote back in its box.

"That bedtime sounded rough. Everything okay?" he asked.

"Owen doesn't do well off schedule," she explained. "He can't moderate his behavior when he's tired or stressed."

"Who can?" Everett said with an easy smile. "My trigger is hunger. You wouldn't want to be near me when I haven't eaten. It's ugly." When she continued to remain in the entryway, he patted the seat beside him.

Tentatively, she stepped forward, sitting a safe distance away. She cleared her throat. "What did you want to talk about? If it's the repayment, I'm sure there's a form for that somewhere on the internet. I can look now if you…" She trailed off when he rested his hand on her forearm.

"It's not about the car, Lissy. I wanted to tell you that I'm done staying out of your life. I've respected your wishes for seven years, but I'm done."

"What wishes?" she said, blinking at him in confusion.

"When I came to see you in the hospital after Owen, you said you wanted me to go away and leave you alone, to stay out of your life."

She cringed at the hurt in his tone. "Everett, I was a terrified kid, and I was humiliated. I didn't want to face your disappointment."

"Disappointment?" He repeated the word as if he'd never heard it before. "How could I be disappointed in you?" He moved closer, sliding his arm to the couch behind her. "It's not the mistakes we make in life that define us; it's our reaction to them, and no one could be a better mom than you are, Liss."

Her eyes welled at the unexpected compliment, but she didn't allow her tears to spill over. Blinking them away, she tried to compose herself. She hadn't realized how much she had been hungering for affirmation until she heard it. Did he really think she was a good mom?

"You really didn't want me out of your life?" he asked.

"No," she said. "I don't even remember saying that." She thought he went away because he was repulsed by her or embarrassed by the situation or afraid of the inevitable questions about Owen's parentage.

Everett looked stunned. "All this time I've let my wounded pride keep me away, and I could have been helping you. I'm sorry, Larissa."

She smiled, turning to face him. "Everett, regardless of what you believe, I am not your responsibility. Maybe I needed these last seven years to learn how to stand on my own without you swooping in to rescue me all the time."

"I like rescuing you," he said, sounding as pouty as Owen did sometimes.

And I like being rescued by you, Larissa thought, shoving away the embarrassing thought before it could cause a blush. "You don't have to rescue me anymore. I'm a capable adult and a mom; I'm the one who does the rescuing now."

"You're a police officer," he said, smiling. "You have no idea how much it makes me smile whenever I see you cruising around town. I'm proud of you."

It was happening again—Larissa's eyes were filling with tears. But no one in her life had ever said those four words to her before. They eased into her heart, filling up the cracks and smoothing over hurts, making all the years of hard work worthwhile. "Thank you," she said, her voice a husky whisper.

They sat in comfortable silence a few minutes until he spoke again. "So we're friends again," he said.

"But, Everett, I meant what I said before. I'm not a little girl anymore. It can't be the same as it was with you in charge and swooping to my rescue all the time. We're equals now."

"Okay."

"And people are going to talk," she added uncomfortably. "About Owen and you. He looks a lot like you."

"Sweetheart, if the worst thing people can say about me is that I fathered a child out of wedlock, then that will be a step up from what they already say about me."

"What do people say about you?" she asked, her tone defensive. Who could dare to say anything bad about Everett?

"Let's say a lot of people find it suspicious that I'm twenty nine and have no interest in dating or settling down."

"You like women," she said, her tone more accusatory than she intended.

"Yes, I do. But a confirmed bachelor in a small town is bound to raise a lot of questions."

"So is a single mother," she said, sighing.

He reached out and took her hand, holding it comfortably in his. "Don't worry about it. People are always going to talk. We know the truth of what's between us."

She nodded, but inside she felt uncertain. What *was* between them? How would their friendship work now? If it looked like dating to the outside world, then was it actually dating? Would there be kissing? What if there was kissing? Was she ready for that? Catching sight of Everett's beautiful profile in her peripheral vision, she thought she could probably make the adjustment.

"What are you going to do now?" he asked.

She jumped, startled from her thoughts of kissing him. "I need to do a load of laundry, scrub the kitchen floor, lay out our clothes for tomorrow, pack the lunches, pay some bills, and set out our breakfast."

"Is that all?" he asked, his tone teasing.

"No," she said seriously. "There's always something that needs done. Why?"

"I was thinking maybe you could sit here and watch the end of the World Series with me."

How was it fair that a man should have such long, thick, charcoal lashes? And how could she resist when he asked her anything? "Okay," she said, feeling like a snake who had been charmed out of its basket.

He smiled, turning on the television again before leaning back, her hand still securely tucked in his. Then he let go her hand and put his arm around her, cinching her close against his side. She had no choice but to rest her head on him. Had he always smelled so good and felt so solid? Unable to resist the urge, she laid her hand on his chest, the comforting rhythm of his heart thumping against her palm. Yes, she could definitely get used to being friends with Everett Honeywell again.

CHAPTER 9

*L*arissa stood on the doorstep, her hands clenched nervously behind
her back. She had never dared approach his house before, feeling
that the hallowed Honeywell borders were too pristine to be sullied
by a mere Porter. But desperate times called for desperate measures, and she
was desperate to see Everett.

*She hadn't seen him in two years since he went away to college. She
hadn't contacted him, though he had sent her the occasional card and some
money. The fact that he was actually thinking of her while he was at his
prestigious university was mind boggling. She had wanted to write, to thank
him or to say hello, but she had been intimidated, feeling oddly shy when she
had never been shy with him before.*

*Now, however, she had to see him and couldn't wait any more. She was
debating knocking on the massive front door again when it was suddenly
opened by a middle-aged woman, Sandy, the Honeywell's housekeeper.*

*"May I help you?" Sandy asked, sweeping an assessing gaze up and down
Larissa.*

*"May I speak with Everett, please? It's an emergency," she added, in case
Sandy was of a mind to deny her request.*

*"Yes of course. Please come in while I fetch him." She stepped aside, but
Larissa remained rooted to the spot.*

"No, thank you, I'll wait out here if that's okay." She had never set foot in the Honeywell house, and she had no intention of changing that today, even though she was curious about the grand house. She'd heard rumors that it was lined with priceless artwork, but she thought that's all they were— rumors. The Honeywells seemed far too down to earth to decorate their home with priceless treasures. They were more the type to frame handmade drawings by their children or grandchildren, if they ever had any. The brothers were taking so much time to settle down that people in town were taking bets about whether or not any of them actually would.

The door closed and Larissa twisted miserably on the step, wishing she could be anywhere else but here. Her eyes darted around the vast and pristine landscape, taking in the acres of white fencing that denoted the Honeywell's property. At this moment, she had never been more ashamed to be a Porter. Her eyes filled with tears, but she blinked them away. It wouldn't do to deliver her message while crying. She would have to do it stoically, like a grownup.

The door opened and she whirled to face Everett. For a few seconds, they surveyed each other in stunned surprise, then he stepped forward with a huge grin and wrapped her in a bear hug.

"Lissy," he said, "I'm so glad to see you." He stepped back, dropping his hands to rest on her shoulders. "Look at you almost all grown up. Fourteen agrees with you."

She smiled, thinking twenty agreed with him, too. He looked the same, yet different somehow. He was the same huge size, but it suited him better now as if he had grown into it. She hadn't noticed him looking like a gangly puppy before he left home, but now that he had filled out some she realized that was probably what he had resembled.

"Come inside," he continued. "You can have a snack and catch me up on what being a freshman in high school is like." He turned to go, but she didn't follow.

"No," she said, her tone more serious than his had been. He paused and turned to look at her in question. "Everett, I have to tell you something." She glanced away, seeking reprieve from his earnest expression. How was she supposed to tell someone so honest and so good something so bad? She cleared *her throat, forcing herself to look him in the eyes again. "You know last month when someone poisoned your horse?"*

Abruptly, his smile fled. He stood straighter, clenching his fist. "Yes," he said, his tone harsh.

She drew in a quavering breath. "That was my brother, Nick. I heard him talking about it with one of his friends. They're coming back tonight for Unbroken Leather."

He went still at the name of the family's most valuable horse. A contender for the Triple Crown, it was worth well over a million dollars. "Why?" he asked in a choked whisper.

"There is no why with him. He's mean and he's jealous. I'm so sorry," she said, her voice breaking on the last word.

Everett's expression cleared and he actually managed a smile. "This isn't your fault, Liss."

"He's my family; I'm so ashamed," she added in a whisper.

"Don't," Everett said. "Don't take responsibility for someone else's bad behavior."

She nodded, biting her lip to keep her tears in check, thinking he shouldn't have to comfort her over this. It should be she who comforted him. He smiled and gave a reassuring pat to her shoulder. "Thanks for coming to tell me," he said. "I would give you a ride home, but I think it's probably better if no one knows you were here. Will you be okay?"

She nodded, sniffling, and then she raised her head, tipping her chin defiantly. "I'll testify if you need me to."

"I appreciate that, Lissy, but we'll see if we can leave you out of it. I have the feeling it wouldn't go well if your family knew you were involved."

She was sure of that fact, but she didn't care. She was doing what was right, and it felt good. "I don't care what happens to me," she said.

"I do. I'll talk to my brothers and the sheriff and we'll see if we can catch him in action tonight so your name never has to be involved." He stepped forward and gave her a quick, one-armed hug. "Thanks."

She smiled, leaning into him for a second, enjoying the warm security of his embrace. When was the last time someone hugged her? She couldn't remember, and suddenly she wasn't sure anyone ever had. "Don't thank me," she said sincerely. She owed him so much more than she could ever repay. He dropped his arm and they took a step apart. He was distracted by the new information and she knew he was longing to call the sheriff and talk to his brothers.

"Goodbye, Everett," she said, taking a step back off the porch. "Have fun back at college." She said the last part a bit wistfully. College was her dream among dreams.

He pulled his thoughts back from wherever they were and smiled at her. "You'll get there someday, Lissy. I'm sure of it. Take care." He smiled again, and that was when it happened; that was when Larissa knew for certain that she loved him. Unable to speak around the new information, she simply nodded, stumbling as she took another step back. His brow lowered in concern as he searched her face. Afraid if he studied her too long he would see the truth of her new feelings, she turned and fled down the long lane, not stopping until she reached her parents' tiny trailer.

CHAPTER 10

The morning brought a new set of problems for Larissa. As Owen got off the bus, she turned to grab her keys and bag when her phone rang. Without checking the caller ID, she pushed the button and heard her brother's voice.

"I need a hundred dollars," he said.

"Sounds like you need a job," Larissa replied, unfazed by his wheedling, demanding tone.

"You know I can't work 'cause of my bad back."

Larissa rolled her eyes. The only thing bad about his back was the lack of use it received from doing any actual labor. It was, however, his convenient excuse for not working and also for his raging drug habit. "I'm not giving you money, Nick. I told you the last time you called and the time before that. I'm not feeding your habit."

"It's not for me; it's for my kids. They're hungry and they need clothes."

"Then bring them over and I'll feed them and buy them clothes," Larissa said. To the outside observer, her attitude might seem calloused, but she knew her brother was lying. She could tell because his mouth was moving.

"They're with their moms. Give me the money and I'll buy the stuff."

"Nice try, Nicky. No money."

"You have plenty for your fancy new car," he said. The bitterness and resentment in his tone was palpable.

"A car that I worked hard for and will be paying off for the next five years. No one handed me that car on a silver platter, Nick. I have a job, a job I'm going to be late for if you don't stop talking."

"What about Mom and Dad? You never help them."

She pinched the bridge of her nose. "Mom and Dad are adults, and so are you. I'm trying to take care of my son who is still a child. I don't know why you believe I have a lot of money, but I don't. I barely have enough to pay my monthly bills."

"Whatever, Larissa. You think you're too good for us, and you always have."

"I'm not having this discussion with you again," Larissa said. Her brother loved to argue about anything and everything and always tried to get a rise out of her. Staying calm was her best defense; it drove him crazy.

With a nasty expletive, he hung up on her. She sighed, tossing the phone into her bag. His voice had sounded frenetic and she wondered if he was using something harder than prescription drugs again. It always amazed her that a person who hadn't worked a day in his life could still afford all the drugs he wanted. *Please don't let it be meth,* she thought.

Like any small, rural community, meth was a huge problem. As a cop, she had seen the effects of all kinds of drugs, but meth was by far the worst. Not only did it render a person physically unrecognizable, but it gave him the strength and energy of ten men, meaning that someone who was high was nearly impossible to take down. Sometimes not even bullets worked to stop users. Thankfully Larissa had never had to shoot anyone. Usually the people she encountered were in the manic phases where they felt euphoric. But she had seen training videos of some of the scarier addicts, and she had learned never to underestimate a user. Reason was meaningless to them.

Pushing away stressful thoughts of her family, she turned her attention to memories of Everett. He hadn't kissed her goodbye, not even on the cheek. Instead, when the game was finished, he had said a cheery farewell and let himself out, locking the door behind him. She wasn't disappointed, per se, but his comforting and overwhelmingly masculine presence had made her realize that something was missing in her life. Maybe it was time to give dating a try. Of course she would have to be careful and not involve Owen until she had vetted the guy, but what would it hurt to go on a few casual dates?

The thought made her both exhilarated and anxious. She had bypassed dating, skipping straight to motherhood without passing "Go." Now to suddenly start dating at twenty three was nerve wracking. What should she wear? What should she say? More important, who should she go out with?

That one, at least, had a possible answer. Detective Calhoun Boyd, Cal to his friends, was new to the area and new to their tiny force. A transplant from Atlanta, he retained all of his southern charm with a hint of big city sophistication. Divorced, he had made no secret of his interest in Larissa. She had put him off, not wanting to date someone with baggage. Who was she kidding, though? Her family was enough baggage for ten people. Cal knew all about her notorious relatives and seemed interested in her anyway. As if fate was sending her a sign, he was also the first person she ran into that morning.

"Officer Porter," he said, smiling so that one of his cheeks dimpled.

"Detective Boyd," she said, smiling in return.

He paused, staring at her in surprise a few beats. Usually she smiled shyly and shuffled away. Larissa scraped her mind to find something suitable to say. From her son, she had learned that sports were always a safe topic with the male persuasion.

"Did you catch the last game of the World Series last night?" she asked.

"I did. Did you?"

"I was on the edge of my seat."

"I didn't take you for a baseball fan," he said.

"I'm not, really. My son is into it, and I was watching with a friend who's a sports enthusiast."

"A sports enthusiast," he repeated. "That's such a girl thing to say." He shook his head, smiling as he rolled his eyes.

"Guess that means I'm a girl," she said. In her head, the comment had sounded flirtatious, but she wasn't sure her delivery was right. Where was her sister, Shelby, when she needed her? *About to have her fifth baby by a fifth different guy,* Larissa thought, her flirtatious smile ebbing. Maybe she was doing the wrong thing. The fear that she would suddenly turn into a serial maneater was never far from her thoughts.

"I guess you are," Cal replied. His tone was neutral, but his look was calculating. Instinctively Larissa knew that this was the beginning of a dance. He was testing the waters, and if she passed the verbal sparring that would occur over their next few meetings then he would ask her out. She also somehow knew she should leave him wanting more.

"See you around, Detective," she said, smiling as she turned and walked away. Maybe all those years sitting at Shelby's knee as she got ready for an endless stream of dates hadn't been for nothing. Larissa felt like there was latent, untapped knowledge brimming somewhere inside her, waiting to be used. Shelby was really good at the beginning part of dating, at hooking a man and reeling him in. The problem came later when she threw herself at him, losing all self respect, allowing herself to be used however he wanted. It never worked, though, the men always walked away, usually leaving her with a child in their absence.

The day was once again mundane, but Larissa felt anxious, as if something big was on its way. Maybe it was her imagination, but it seemed like a few quiet days in a row were usually followed by an explosion of activity. Last time it had been like this she had gone to work on a Friday, expecting another quiet day. Instead there had been a domestic situation where the husband was holding his wife hostage at gunpoint and the SWAT team from Lexington had been called in to diffuse the situation. That was the way it went with police work—a good officer was prepared to handle any situation at a moment's notice. And sometimes even the most innocuous situation could turn suddenly volatile. Keeping a cool, rational head was vitally important.

Larissa smiled when her day ended and she traded her cruiser for her beautiful new car. "Hello, beautiful," she whispered, realizing for the first time why some people loved their cars so much. Without a doubt, this was the nicest car she had ever owned. And she had to agree with her son—red was the best color. Growing up, her family had only occasionally owned a vehicle. Either her parents' licenses were suspended or their cars were repossessed. Larissa had learned from an early age the best way to spot and dodge a repo man.

She had only owned one car, the same jalopy she had disposed of, and it had never engendered any feelings of love, only despair and frustration. But this car, without any rust or dings, lessened the feeling of insecurity when she drove up the Honeywell's long lane. Maybe she still didn't belong, but she was closer than she had been before.

Today Owen was waiting for her and brimming with excitement. "Mom, Mom, a horse foaled today and it was awesome," he yelled as he burst from one of the beautiful white barns, skidding to a stop beside her car.

"You watched?" she asked, not sure how she felt about that. Not that she wanted to keep him from witnessing the miracle of life, but she wasn't ready for the inevitable questions such an event would bring.

He nodded, twisting his face into a grimace. "It was disgusting."

She laughed and so did Everett who sauntered out from the barn, wiping his hands on a towel. "Want to come and see?" Everett offered.

Larissa nodded, smiling. Owen grasped her hand, tugging her forward when he felt she was walking too slowly. They came to a stop beside a pen, heady with the scent of new hay. "Oh, it just happened," Larissa said, noting the wetness behind the foal's ears as his mother fervently licked him clean.

"You barely missed it," Everett said.

"Don't feel too bad, Mom," Owen said. "I don't think it was something a girl should watch."

She laughed again. At least when she told him how he came into the world he would have some understanding and appreciation of what she had gone through.

"Girls are stronger than you think sometimes," Everett added, resting his hand comfortably on Owen's shoulder. "And your Mom is the strongest one I know."

Owen looked at her as she stared at the foal, blushing. "But she's so small. I'm almost as tall as she is."

"There are different kinds of strength," Everett said. "I'm talking about the kind you can't see."

"Thanks, Everett," Larissa mumbled.

In return, he smiled. "Why don't you stay for supper tonight, Liss?"

"Oh, I don't..." she trailed off, helpless to find an appropriate excuse to say no.

"Can we, Mom? Can we please, please, please?" Owen begged, his hands clasped pleadingly in front of his chest. "I want to see the new foal again later when he's all cleaned up. Please?"

"Owen, I don't think..." She trailed off again when Everett interrupted.

"Come on, Larissa. We've been friends for seventeen years. I think it's about time you met my family."

Larissa felt like she might hyperventilate. Facing all the Honeywells at once? And over dinner in their beautiful house? It was too much. "Everett," she began tentatively. And then she looked up into his beautiful black eyes and knew she would say yes, especially when he reached out and clasped her hand.

"Please," he said.

"Okay," she said, thinking she would agree to anything when he looked at her like that and said "please."

He smiled, squeezing her hand. "I'll go tell my mother and come back for you," he said.

"I don't want to make trouble by adding guests at the last minute," Larissa said.

"Honey, this is Kentucky—we live to add guests at the last minute," Everett said, turning to go toward the house. Owen started to follow him, but Larissa held him back, clutching his shoulder as she bent to whisper in his ear.

"Owen, I want you on your best behavior, do you understand? Company manners with all the pleases and thank yous. Put your napkin in your lap, speak when you're spoken to, smile, and eat in small bites."

Owen squirmed under her tight embrace. "Ow, Mom, you're hurting me."

"I want to make sure you're on your very best behavior tonight. I mean it, Owen. If I have to punish you for anything, you're going to get double."

"I'll be good," Owen promised, attempting to writhe out of her clasp again. Larissa realized she was projecting her anxiety onto her son and took a breath.

"I know you'll be good," she said, taking a deep breath. "You're a good boy, and I'm proud of you."

Owen nodded, looking more relaxed. "What's the big deal, Mom? It's only the Honeywells."

Larissa laughed out loud at that, glad her son had no idea that the Honeywells were the closest thing to royalty their community had to offer. When she was growing up, she had heard a lot about the high and mighty Honeywells from her parents who spewed their bitterness at anyone who had more than they did. No wonder her siblings had followed suit. If Everett hadn't conveniently inserted himself into her life, would their resentment have rubbed off on her? If she didn't know what good, honest, and generous people the Honeywells were, would she think they were rich snobs like many people in the town did? She wasn't sure, but she did know that she was in awe of Mr. and Mrs. Honeywell and desperate to make a good impression.

Everett returned to retrieve them, and Larissa was glad. She couldn't imagine walking into the grand house unaccompanied. Maybe she was building them up in her head too much. They had raised Everett, after all, and he had no trouble accepting the fact that she was a Porter.

Sensing her hesitation, he took hold of her hand, resting his free hand on Owen's shoulder. When he gave her hand a squeeze, she smiled up at him, her heart contracting painfully with the realization that her love for him had never dimmed; it had simply moved to the background while she made Owen her first priority. And now that Everett was back, it was impossible to ignore. He wanted nothing more than friendship from her, though. He had made that perfectly clear seven years ago, and he felt the same way now.

He let go her hand and slipped his arm around her shoulders, giving her a squeeze. "Lissy, you look like you're marching to your death sentence," he whispered. "It's my parents; they're going to love you."

She bit her lip, hoping it was true, and then they came face to face with his mother. At first the older woman was smiling politely in welcome, and then her eyes slid to Owen and lingered, frozen in speculation. Larissa watched as her gaze shifted from Owen to Everett and back again, taking in their similar hair and eye color. If Everett noticed, he was oblivious.

"Mom, this is Larissa Porter, and this is Owen." He gave Owen's shoulder a light squeeze. Larissa heard the note of pride in his voice, and knew his mother noticed it, too. "Larissa and Owen, this is my mother."

At last Mrs. Honeywell ripped her eyes off Owen and held out her hand to Larissa. "How do you do, Larissa? I'm very pleased you could join us tonight." Larissa could tell she was trying to keep her eyes off Owen, but she couldn't quite manage it, shooting him studying looks every few seconds as she waited for Larissa to respond.

"Mrs. Honeywell, thank you for having me. Your home is lovely."

Mrs. Honeywell gave her an absent smile. "Thank you, dear." Once the polite exchange was over, she turned her full attention to Owen, holding out her hand to him. "How do you do, Owen?"

"Ma'am," Owen replied, shaking her hand. Larissa sighed in relief that, so far, his manners were impeccable.

"How old are you?" Mrs. Honeywell asked, more intensity creeping into her tone.

"I'm seven, ma'am, and I'm in first grade this year. How old are you?"

"Owen," Larissa snapped.

He looked at her in question. "What? You told me to ask people questions about themselves."

Fortunately, Mrs. Honeywell had a sense of humor after raising so many sons. "You did the right thing by asking me a question, Owen, it's that you accidently raised the one question you're never supposed to ask a lady. We don't like to say how old we are."

"But the girls in my class all tell me they're seven," he said, perplexed.

"Well, after seven we start to be a little more coy. Would you like to try another question?"

He bit his lip, searching around the room while Larissa held her breath. The longer he thought, the more time he had to come up with something embarrassing. "Have you ever seen a horse have her baby? 'Cause I saw that today."

Larissa let out the breath she had been holding. Horses were a safe topic here.

Mrs. Honeywell nodded, smiling. "I have seen that a few times. It's very exciting, isn't it?"

"Yes, ma'am," Owen said.

"Maybe you'd like to name the new foal," Mrs. Honeywell suggested.

Owen gasped as if he had been granted the keys to the kingdom. He looked to Larissa for affirmation. "Can I, Mom? Can I please?"

"If Mrs. Honeywell says so, then you may," Larissa replied, smiling gratefully at Everett's mother.

Mrs. Honeywell returned her smile, though it looked slightly strained. "He's very tall for seven, isn't he?" she asked, darting a glance at Everett—all 6'11" of him.

Larissa cleared her throat, shifting uncomfortably. "Yes, ma'am, he's tall for his age." She suddenly felt very conspicuous and awkward as she pitched about for a topic change. "I apologize for wearing my uniform. If I had known...well, I would have brought clothes to change into."

Mrs. Honeywell's smile was genuine and untroubled now as she waved her hand dismissively in front of her face. "Don't give it a thought, dear. It's nice to see an officer in the house when she's not here to arrest one of my sons. In fact, this may be a first. Follow me, please," she said, and then she led the way into the dining room.

They walked into the dining room where all the other Honeywells and their wives were already seated. All of them came to a halt and stared at Larissa and Owen, and then from Owen to Everett and back again.

"Hey, it's Officer Porter," Grant said, giving her a friendly and enthusiastic wave. "The charges against me were dropped."

"I'm glad," she said. His smile was infectious and she found her mood lightening. Everett took over then and made the introductions to his father, oldest brother, Brent, his wife, Haley, the next brother in line, Corliss, and his wife, Allie.

"Darcy and Genevieve are back at their farm," Everett explained. "They come and go, and then of course Ivy's in Montana." She couldn't miss the derisive note in his tone when he talked about Montana, but Larissa was glad Ivy had gotten away from Kentucky. Though four years ahead of her in school, Ivy had always reminded Larissa of a fragile butterfly, trapped in a too-small jar. Montana seemed far enough removed from her brothers' overprotective influence that she could finally spread her wings and fly free.

"Nice to meet you all," Larissa uttered shyly, resisting the urge to duck behind Everett.

The family echoed some form of return greeting, and they were finally able to sit. Mr. Honeywell said the blessing, and the food began to pass. Larissa had seen Thanksgiving episodes of television shows that reminded her of the scene she was now witnessing—a bountiful harvest for a treasure trove of family members. But this was apparently what every day was like here. No wonder none of the brothers wanted to leave home; it was like paradise.

Occasionally, one of the brothers or their wives directed gentle questions at Owen, who handled them with aplomb, answering politely and loud enough to be understood in the large room. Larissa's heart was practically bursting with pride at this first real test of his manners. Then he started to squirm with an expression she knew well. After staring helplessly around the large room, he finally leaned over to whisper in her ear.

"Mom, I need to be excused for a couple of minutes, please. It's urgent."

Everett, overhearing, leaned over to whisper directions to the bathroom. Larissa watched as he quietly pushed back from the table and laid his napkin on his chair. Everett was watching, too. He and Larissa locked eyes, smiling, and he winked. Her moment of happiness was short lived, however, because as soon as Owen was safely out of the room, Mrs. Honeywell spoke.

"Forgive my manners, but I'm going to address the elephant in the room here. Is Owen Everett's son or not?"

CHAPTER 11

"*Larissa, you never go out.*"

"*That's because I'm always studying or working,*" Larissa replied, tugging on the uncomfortable pants. They were Angie's pants, and they were a little too tight, but they were new and far better than anything she owned.

"*I'm saying that it's time you gave yourself a break and enjoyed life for once,*" Angie said. "*Shove all thoughts of work and school from your mind for once.*"

"*I'll try,*" Larissa said unconvincingly, but she had a big test on Monday that she wanted to spend the weekend prepping for. Angie, however, was her first friend—her only friend—and she didn't want to let her down the one time she asked her to go out.

"*This party is down your alley,*" Angie told her. "*It's supposed to be tame, and it's going to be filled with college guys.*"

"*If it's going to be filled with college guys, then how can it be tame?*" Larissa asked. At sixteen she realized that older guys were notorious party animals, at least the ones Shelby dated were.

"*They're like smart, or something. I don't know; it's some sort of fraternity thing.*"

"*Then why would they ever let us in?*" Larissa asked.

"*Because they're not going to know we're only sixteen,*" Angie said.

"*I'm not going to lie,*" Larissa said.

"*You won't have to. No one is going to ask. Believe me, I got a good line on this party from my brother's friend. There aren't going to be a ton of girls there, and they'll be happy for any who show up. This isn't going to be a beer fest; it's a gentle get together. My brother didn't even give me a hard time about coming.*"

There was a look on Angie's face that Larissa recognized, sort of a wistful longing that she used whenever she talked about her brother's best friend. "Is he going to be there?" Larissa asked.

"*Who?*"

"*You know who,*" Larissa said, poking her in the rib.

Angie writhed away with a laugh. "Okay, you caught me. Max is going to be there, but I'm not going to talk to him." She struck a haughty pose with her nose in the air.

Sure you're not, Larissa thought. Angie was helpless to resist Max, and no wonder. He was as cute as he was sweet. It was Larissa's secret opinion that Max liked Angie as much as Angie liked Max, but she didn't say anything because she didn't want to give her friend false hope. What did she know about dating? She was in love with a man she hadn't seen in two long years, a man too old for her who saw her as nothing but a child—someone so far out of her reach he was practically a fantasy.

"*Here we are,*" *Angie announced, her nervous tone causing Larissa's stomach to clench with terror of her own. She was in Lexington, half an hour from their small town of Silver Springs. But what if it wasn't far enough to escape her family's reputation? What if she saw someone who recognized the name Porter and all associated with it? What if people expected her to be like Shelby or their older sister, Tonya? She shouldn't have come here; she should have stayed home and studied; there was no way to get in trouble while studying in the safety of her bedroom, especially since Nick had gone to juvenile detention. Maybe it was disloyal to think so, but the trailer was much more peaceful without him, almost like a real home for once with Larissa and her little sister and brother left. Fortunately they preferred to be out in the community wreaking havoc instead of staying home and causing a disruption. Her parents had also begun to slow down on their partying. Some week-*

ends it was only the three of them on a Friday night, with Larissa reading a book while her parents watched television, like any normal family.

"There he is," Angie hissed, clutching Larissa's hand. Larissa looked up to see Max eyeing them from across the room. She tried to smile at him, but he had eyes only for Angie. "He's coming over," Angie added, sounding frantic.

Larissa gave her hand a squeeze. "Relax. You've got this."

Angie nodded, swallowing convulsively, but by the time Max arrived in front of them she had composed her face into a relaxed smile. "Max, what are you doing here?"

Larissa had to bite her lip to hide her smile because her friend's surprise sounded genuine, as if she hadn't planned this evening hoping to run into him. He must have been thinking the same thing because he gave her a wry smile.

"I was wondering the same thing about you, Ang, although I could have sworn you were standing right there when I told your brother about this party."

"Was that where I heard about it?" Angie asked with mock innocence as she surveyed the room. "I'm a little disappointed, though. I thought this was going to be a rager, and you know how I like a good party."

He laughed. "Right, Miss Goody-Goody. I'm surprised to see you at a party that's even this tame, but it's about time you got out away from your overprotective big brother."

"What's wrong with my brother?" she asked, her tone defensive.

"Nothing. He's my best friend, and that's the problem. C'mon, let's dance." He took her hand, not waiting for a reply. She trotted helplessly behind him, throwing Larissa a delighted glance over her shoulder. Larissa smiled as she watched them, enjoying the scene as if it were a play. Angie was the nicest girl she knew, and she was a little amazed that she was willing to be friends with her. Kids at school were standoffish, as if being close to a Porter might somehow sully their good name, even though Larissa was quiet, clean, and well-behaved. Angie had been the only person to cross the gap. The only person except one, Larissa amended. Everett had been her first friend, her only friend for a long time.

Her thoughts turned melancholy as she wondered what he was up to. He would be graduating soon and then he would come home. Her heart beat fast with that thought. Their town was small. Surely she would run into him occasionally, wouldn't she? And when she did, he would have to see that she wasn't a baby anymore, wouldn't he? Could he actually like her in that way? She knew he never had because by now she knew the signals a man put off when he liked a woman. To Everett, she was a child, and a needy one at that. But Larissa was becoming a woman who needed him in different ways.

"That's a serious face for a party." The words jolted her, startling her so that she jumped. Had she been thinking so hard of Everett that she imagined him talking to her now? Was she going crazy? But when his face split into a welcoming smile, she knew it was him.

"Everett!" she exclaimed. Discarding her usual reserve, she threw her arms around him. Belatedly she realized what she had done and wondered if he would mind, but must not have because he returned her hug with equal fervor.

"Lissy, what are you doing here?" he asked. After bestowing a bear hug that lifted her feet from the floor, he set her down and inspected her from head to toe.

"I came with a friend." She pointed around him toward Angie and Max who were swaying slowly and staring dreamily into each other's eyes.

Everett turned to look, frowning. "Him or her?"

"Her," she said.

He nodded, his smile resuming as he studied her again. "Look at you, all grown up."

She tried not to be disheartened by his paternal tone. Obviously he wasn't going to be love struck at the first sight of her, but these things took time. She could be patient. "You're graduating soon," she said for lack of something better.

"Five weeks," he said, his tone excited.

"Haven't you enjoyed college?" she asked. To her, college was a magical place—far from her family and full of learning.

"It's been interesting. I guess I'm sort of a homebody, though." His smile turned sheepish, as if revealing the fact that he loved his family was somehow shameful.

"I would be, too, if I lived in your home," she blurted, embarrassed at her hasty words.

Everett laughed, though. "So maybe when I get home I'll invite you up sometime."

She blinked at him. Was he flirting with her? The words were innocuous, but there was something subtle in his tone. As if having the same realization, he tore his attention from her and surveyed the room. "I should probably go," he said.

"No," she blurted again, laying her hand on his forearm. Where was her filter tonight? Surely she wasn't going to beg Everett Honeywell to stay with her, was she? "One dance?" she said, trying to keep the desperate hope out of her tone.

He looked down at her, and she could see the conflict in his eyes as he debated the appropriateness of one dance with her.

"It's a party, Everett," she added, purposely making her tone matter of fact to alleviate any doubts about her intentions.

His expression cleared and he gave her a sunny smile. "Okay, let's dance," he said. Clasping her hand, he led her behind him to the makeshift dance floor before turning to take her in his arms. She thought his mother would be proud because, if the three inch gap between their bodies was any indication, he was leaving plenty of room for the Holy Ghost.

"I'm not so great at dancing," he said. "Too tall."

She was surprised to realize he meant it, and it was a revelation. Everett was insecure about some things. Who knew? Certainly not Larissa who had always thought him invincible. Instead of turning her off, though, she found the news of his humanity reassuring. Maybe he wasn't totally out of reach. Maybe he was a real person, like her. "Are you dating anyone at school?" she asked, blushing crimson after the words left her mouth. What was her problem tonight? Where was her finesse? Oh, that's right; she didn't have any.

Everett chuckled, a soft sound that rumbled in his stomach. "No. I told you before that dating isn't for me. I prefer to remain happily single, thank you very much. Women are very nice and very pretty, but they tend to take over. No offense."

"None taken," Larissa said, though she didn't really mean it. How could she not be offended by the news that Everett wanted nothing to do with her?

Maybe he didn't mean it. Maybe he simply hadn't found the right woman and fallen in love. Maybe he needed a little convincing.

"What's that smile for?" he asked.

"I was wondering if you'll ever change your mind," she said. "Maybe you'll meet the right person and fall head over heels in love with her, so much so that you beg her to marry you."

He laughed again. "My little Liss is turning into a romantic. I like that. You should hold out for the fairy tale."

"Why shouldn't you?" she pressed, knowing she should let it go but feeling powerless to do so. "You're some girl's Prince Charming, Everett. Why deny it?"

"I'm glad you think so," he said, sidestepping her question.

"You've been a good friend to me over the years," she said. "The best."

In response, he pulled her slightly closer so their bodies were now actually almost touching. She was tempted to keep talking to see if it might work to close even more of the distance between them.

"How's school?" he asked.

"I'm still the big loser who thinks school is the greatest place on earth," she said, causing his smile to deepen until his cheek dimpled. She stared at the dimple in fascination. How had she missed it before now? "If someone gave me the choice between Disneyworld and a final exam, I'd take the exam hands down. I'm such a hopeless nerd, Everett."

"You're not a hopeless anything. School is a safe place where you excel."

"Wait, I thought you were an architect. When did you switch your major to psych?"

His jaw dropped. "Larissa, are you making fun of me?"

"A little," she said, glancing shyly up at him to make sure she hadn't actually offended him. When he cinched her slightly closer she had her answer. The adjustment in their positions meant she needed to rearrange her hands, sliding them from his biceps to his chest.

His look became owlish as he studied her with wide eyes, blinking slowly. "I should probably not be doing this."

"Why not?" she asked, her soft tone matching his near whisper.

"You're sixteen," he pointed out.

"We're two old friends dancing, Everett. Nothing wrong with that."

"Something tells me I should not be taking reassurances from you," he said, but he made no move to let her go. The song switched to a fast one, but their pace didn't change. Instead they remained swaying slowly together at the edge of the dance floor, at least until Angie interrupted by tapping Larissa's shoulder.

"Will you wait?" Larissa asked, looking up to try and see in his eyes.

His expression was neutral, and her heart began to sink until he answered. "I'll wait," he said.

She smiled, easing away from him to talk to her friend. Angie grabbed her hand and practically dragged her down the hall toward the bathroom. "Was that a Honeywell?" Angie hissed.

Larissa nodded. "That's Everett. We're friends."

"Okay, wow, shocking. You're good with secrets, Larissa. Later, I'm going to drag that whole story out of you, but right now I was wondering if you minded if I took off." She bit her lip and looked hopefully at Larissa.

"You're leaving?" Larissa asked.

Angie nodded. "Max wants to grab a coffee and talk. I was going to offer to take you home but," she paused, glancing at Everett over Larissa's shoulder. "It looks like you're doing well here. Can he give you a ride home?"

"I'm sure he can," Larissa said, tamping down her own excitement. Everett wouldn't refuse her a ride, and that would give them an entire half hour alone in his car. The possibilities were endless. "Have fun with Max. I want details."

"A lady doesn't kiss and tell," Angie said seriously before dissolving in a fit of giggles. "Who am I kidding? I'll give you the complete play by play, and I want to hear yours, too." She glanced again in Everett's direction. "A Porter and a Honeywell. That has Romeo and Juliet written all over it." Then, realizing that she might have offended Larissa by commenting on her family, she gave her hand an apologetic squeeze. "I'm sorry, Larissa. I didn't mean anything by that."

"It's okay," Larissa said, trying to believe the words. "I know it's an impossible dream. Everett and I are friends."

"If the way he was holding you and looking at you was any indication, I'd say you're a whole lot more than that," Angie said. Reaching forward, she

gave Larissa a tight, quick hug. "Details," she whispered again before turning and scurrying toward the door.

Larissa watched her go with a sad smile. She wished she could believe Angie's words about Everett's feelings being more than friendship. Unfortunately it was her other words that lodged in her head. A Porter and a Honeywell. The two names could barely be said in the same sentence. The families were opposite in every way. The only thing they had in common was the fact that they lived in the same town and had a large number of children. Otherwise they might as well have been different species. The Honeywells with their proud heritage, scads of money, high morals, and impressive house were a family to be admired. The Porters, on the other hand, could only trace their family back two generations to the first illegitimate son of a murderer. From there, the family's history had only gone downhill. What little money they had was spent on temporary fixes to try and make life bearable. They had the morals of a rutting pig, and the stench to match. No, there was no way the two families would ever combine. Generations of Honeywells would roll over in their graves.

"What's wrong?" Everett asked as soon as she returned.

"Nothing. I..." To her horror, her eyes filled with tears. Shaking her head, she turned and sprinted toward the door and freedom. If only she could get a little fresh air, then maybe she could clear her head.

Of course Everett followed, though. There was no possibility for a clear head as long as he was around. "Larissa," he said, laying a gentle hand on her shoulder as soon as they reached the porch. Surprisingly, they had the porch to themselves. The mellow strains of music filtered from the inside, cocooning them in the dark intimacy of the portico. "What's wrong? Did your friend upset you?"

She shook her head, squeezing her eyes tight to blink back the tears. "You must think I'm crazy," she said, aiming to make light of the situation.

"I think no such thing," Everett said solemnly. "I think you're amazing."

She turned to look up at him. "You do?"

He nodded, dropping his hand. "For you to have survived your upbringing is miraculous, but you haven't merely survived. You've thrived. You're smart, sweet, wholesome, and pretty." He added the last wordy shyly, dropping his gaze to the porch floor.

Larissa knew she should close her mouth, but she couldn't quite manage. Everett thought all those things about her? "But I'm a Porter," she said.

He looked up at her then, his expression fierce. "Your name means nothing more than what you do with it," he said. "It wouldn't matter at all that I'm a Honeywell if I chose to live my life in a way that brought dishonor to my family. It's the choices we make that determine our outcome, Larissa, not the name we're born with."

"You really believe that," she said. "It doesn't matter to you at all that I'm a Porter?"

"That's not completely true; knowing you're a Porter helps me understand how much you've had to overcome. But you're doing it, Lissy. You're amazing."

There was that word again, and this time it was accompanied by his fingers brushing her waist. Larissa couldn't quite wrap her mind around the unexpected turn of events, even though it was what she had hoped for. Everett thought she was amazing, and he was touching her, not at all like the big brother he had set himself up as all those years ago.

His fingers remained uncertainly on her waist. She watched his expression close as common sense returned. He was about to withdraw his hand when she spoke. "Kiss me, Everett."

Instead of spurring him on, the plea had the opposite effect. He dropped his hand and took a step back. "No. You're sixteen. I'm twenty two. This whole night has been..." he shook his head, looking suddenly frustrated. "What am I doing?" He pressed his hand to his forehead. "I'm sorry, Larissa. Let's go back to the way it was, okay? Can we pretend none of this ever happened, that I didn't almost lose my mind and cross a line I should never have crossed?"

She licked her lips, studying his hopeful, baleful look, teetering on the edge of something monumental. Should she do what he wanted—what was probably best for both of them—or should she do what she wanted and continue on the path of certain doom? Before she could think about it too much, she stood on her toes, plunged her fingers into his hair, and drew his face down to hers, kissing him. She had never kissed anyone before, so she had no idea if she was doing it correctly, but she must have done something right because Everett responded as if he had been starving for her touch.

The height difference was awkward, but it didn't last for long because he lifted her, pressing her into the porch as he kissed her and then kissed her again. The kiss that had started so intently was quickly spiraling out of their control. Larissa felt both terrified and exhilarated when she could feel anything at all except the rush of sensation Everett was creating. She had no idea it would be like this, and she was glad she hadn't known sooner. She was glad Everett was the first to make her feel so off kilter and out of control.

"Whoa, looks like the party's out here," someone said as he opened the door and walked by, staring unabashedly at the show Larissa and Everett were inadvertently putting on display.

As if snapping free from a spell, Everett came to, dropping Larissa so she slid down the side of the house. "Oh, no, I..." He backed away, looking horrified. "This is so far over the line, I can't even...I never meant to...I'm sorry, Larissa. I'm so sorry." He choked on the last word before he turned and literally sprinted away from her as fast as his long legs would carry him.

Larissa stood staring after him in a daze. For a long while, the only thing she felt was the loss of his physical presence that had somehow been imprinted on her. Though the night was warm, she felt cold, and she shivered. As her rational mind began to return, so did the realization that she had no way to get home.

Breathing shakily, trying to gain a little bit of stability, she turned and wobbled to the house. She had to find a phone, but then what? Certainly no one in her family would come and get her. Angie was her only friend, and she didn't have a cell phone. Larissa would have to call a taxi, but the half hour ride to Silver Springs would bankrupt her. She sighed; it had to be done, though.

"You okay?" A voice spoke somewhere to her right. Her heart clenched; through her fog, the speaker looked like Everett. Had he come back? But, no, it wasn't Everett. He looked enough like him to be related, though--tall, broad-shouldered with thick black hair and dark eyes.

"Are you a Honeywell?" Larissa asked, dazed.

The man smiled. "I don't think so, but then I don't know what one is. Is that a Lexington thing?"

"You don't know who the Honeywells are?" she asked, the surprise pulling her out of her fog. She thought everyone everywhere knew the Honeywells.

The guy shook his head, smiling in amusement. "I'm not from around here," he explained. "I'm on a break from school and visiting my cousin. Where do you go?"

Larissa blinked at him; he thought she was in college? For some reason, she didn't want him to know differently. "I go to community college," she said, the lie tasting sour on her tongue.

He nodded. "You here alone?"

"I wasn't, but I guess I am now," she said uncertainly.

"I could give you a ride," he offered, sidling closer.

Alarm bells began to ring in Larissa's head. "No, thank you."

The guy smiled. "Smart girl. You should never accept a ride with a stranger."

"Then why did you offer?" she asked.

"Because I'm not a stranger to me," he said, smiling at his illogical statement. "How are you going to get home?"

"I'll call a cab," she said, attempting to sound very grownup and nonchalant.

He nodded. "Why don't you have one dance with me before you go?"

"I don't know," she said, darting an uncertain look toward the dance floor. The party was starting to clear out. She should really go home.

"One dance," he pled. "I haven't danced with anyone all night, and you're the prettiest girl in the room."

It was a line, and not even a very good one, but Larissa was desperate enough to find it consoling. Maybe Everett didn't want her, but someone thought she was pretty. "One dance," she agreed, allowing him to take her hand and lead her forward.

They danced a gentle slow dance together, neither of them talking. He was studying her intently, his eyes kindling with interest, but she didn't return his look. He was older and attractive and she was flattered. Her kiss with Everett, though, had ruined her chances with anyone else, maybe ever again. The song ended and she pulled away. "Thanks for the dance," she said.

He nodded, smiling. "Why don't I grab you a soda and then we'll find a phone so you can call a cab?"

The mention of a soda made her realize she was parched. "A soda sounds nice," she said. He left to retrieve it and she stared helplessly around the room. If she were a phone, where would she be?

The guy returned with her soda. He had opened it for her, and she took a sip, grimacing slightly as she looked at the can. Diet, she thought. That must account for the odd flavor. She always drank regular.

"Sorry, was diet not right?" he asked, his tone apologetic. "The girls I know are always obsessing over their weight and only drink diet."

"Diet's fine," she said, sipping absently as she began inspecting the room again. "Where do you think the phone is?"

"I saw it in the kitchen," he said. "Finish up your soda and we can throw the can away when we go in."

Larissa laughed. "Conscientious, aren't you?"

"I do what I can to keep our planet clean." The calculating look was back and it made Larissa uncomfortable. She would be glad to get away from him, but it looked like she wasn't going anywhere until she finished the disgusting soda. Diet was definitely not her thing. Tipping the can back, she chugged it.

"Let's go find that phone now," she said as she crushed the can in her hand. They walked into the kitchen, and that was the last thing she remembered as the world began to tilt and spin. She looked up at the guy helplessly, realizing as she wanted to call for him that she didn't know his name. "What's your..." she began, and then everything went black.

*L*arissa gave Everett a helpless look before opening her mouth to reply. His mother's question hung heavily in the silence of the grand dining room. Thankfully, Everett rescued her.

"Mother, what a question," he said, his light tone helping to clear the atmosphere. He rested his hand on Larissa's knee and gave it a squeeze as he smiled, effectively ending the conversation. His mother wisely retreated behind her curiosity, left to speculate if she'd had her first grandchild seven years ago.

Larissa felt awkward and guilty over the uncertainty, knowing that such a possibility was a stain on the Honeywell family name. Having a child out of wedlock might be commonplace for the Porters, but such a thing had never happened to the Honeywells.

"I'm sorry if that seemed abrupt or disapproving, Larissa," Mrs. Honeywell continued, her tone contrite. "That's not how I meant it. I'm sure you can understand my shock at seeing someone who looks so much like Everett..." She trailed off, biting her lip as she realized she wasn't making the situation any less awkward.

Larissa started to speak again, to tell her the truth about Owen's father, but Everett squeezed her knee again, giving his head a slight shake. And since it was his mother, she deferred to him. Maybe

Everett wanted to explain the situation in private. If so, that was fine with Larissa. She wasn't anxious to announce to the entire table that she had no idea what her son's father's name was, that she had been assaulted on the one night she actually cut loose and went to a party. She didn't think she would ever forgive herself for her stupidity in allowing herself to be such easy prey, but at least she had gotten Owen from her ordeal.

Since neither Larissa nor Everett said anything to fill the awkward silence, Mrs. Honeywell took a breath, preparing to try again, but her husband preempted her. "I think what my wife is trying to say, Larissa, is that we're surprised, but not unhappy. Owen seems like a wonderful little boy, and we're willing to accept the situation, whatever it might be."

"Thank you, Mr. Honeywell," Larissa managed. She wasn't sure what else to say, and she felt suddenly confused, especially when Everett let go her knee and rested his arm on the back of her chair, his fingers curving possessively around her shoulder. It was almost like he wanted his parents to believe that he and Larissa were together and that Owen was his, though she knew that couldn't be; he had insisted that they were friends. He had told her—repeatedly—that he had no desire for a wife or family because he didn't want his life to change. So why the charade? Was it for her benefit, to offer support?

"How did you two meet?" Haley asked, filling the unbearable quiet with a question that was easy to answer. Once again, though, Everett surprised Larissa by answering for her.

"We met at school," Everett said, turning to give Larissa a smile she didn't understand. "She was six and a little wisp of a thing, all big brown eyes and long russet hair."

She was amazed by the way he made her sound desirable, as if she had been the picture of girlish innocence when, in reality, she'd been covered in a layer of dirt, had tear streaked cheeks and a runny nose, and probably smelled bad, too. "You were so tall; I thought you were a teacher," she added.

"And then you found out I was something worse. I'll never forget the way you said 'You're a Honeywell,'" his voice rose to imitate hers, and he wrinkled his nose the way she sometimes did when she was disgusted.

"I didn't think you were worse than a teacher," she said, exasperated. "I couldn't believe you were talking to me."

"You looked so sad. It broke my heart, Liss."

Her heart wasn't broken now. Instead it began to race as his eyes held hers, and then Grant spoke.

"And you never mentioned her in all these years," he said. "It figures. Maybe I should start asking Larissa what's going on in your world, Everett, because it sounds like you talk to her more than you talk to us." Grant sounded like he was half joking and half peeved. Larissa knew the brothers were close. She wondered if it was unusual that Everett hadn't shared any information about her with them, or if they simply chalked it up to his quietness and reserve.

"I haven't talked to her in seven years," Everett said, tearing his eyes from Larissa to look at his brother. "Until recently. Guess I have you to thank for that."

"You could have told me before I asked her out," Grant said, causing Larissa to squirm uncomfortably in her seat. Everett laughed, however.

"Yeah? You asked her out? What'd she say?" he said.

"She said no because she's not allowed to date people she arrests. Though now I'm wondering if that was the real reason," Grant said, giving Larissa a speculative glance.

"That was the real reason," she said, more defensive than she intended. She didn't care for the way they were causally discussing her love life over the dinner table as if she weren't there. Thankfully Owen returned and the conversation turned to something else.

With the return of Owen came the loss of Everett's hand; he removed it casually as he turned to watch Owen walk into the room, and Larissa appreciated his thoughtfulness. She really, really didn't want to have to explain to her son why Everett was touching her shoulder at the dinner table. For now he seemed to accept the fact that Everett was an old friend and nothing more, but if he saw them touching, he would no doubt start to ask if Everett could be his dad again.

Somehow, despite the brief awkwardness, the remainder of supper was pleasant. Maybe it was because Everett and his brothers kept up a lively discussion about the upcoming football season, involving Owen as if he were their equal. For Owen, who loved sports and craved male bonding time, the evening was probably perfect, and that made Larissa happy.

She was still smiling when Everett's mother hugged her goodbye. "Honestly, Larissa, we're happy to have met you and Owen. If you take anything away from this evening, please let that be it," the older women whispered as she held Larissa close.

For Larissa, who had never received a hug or gentle touch from her own mother, the moment was almost too much. She swallowed a lump and nodded her head, hoping her smile conveyed her pleasure at the words.

Everett rested his hand gently on the small of her back, steering her toward the door. She opened the passenger door of her car for Owen, closing it after he was safely buckled inside, and then she turned to Everett.

"What was that about tonight?" she whispered.

"I think we should get our story straight before we figure out what to tell people," he whispered.

"What story?" she asked. "We don't have a story."

"Sure we do," he said. "And people are going to make their own assumptions once they see the three of us together in public."

"We'll be together in public?" she asked, taken aback.

Everett chuckled. "Of course we will, Liss, unless you intend to keep me buried under a rock."

Larissa was confused. Things were sounding very much like they were a couple. "When will we go out?" she asked.

He shrugged. "I don't know. Are you free tomorrow?"

"To do what?"

"Go to a restaurant," he said. "That seems like an innocuous public outing."

Public outing of what? "Everett, I don't know how to ask tactfully, so I'll come right out and say it. Is it a date?"

"You know how I feel about dating, Liss. Of course it's not. It's two old friends going to dinner together. Men and women can be friends."

"You might want to tell Silver Springs, Kentucky, because I'm not sure they've received that memo. People are going to talk. Especially when they see you with Owen."

"People will speculate, but it's none of their business. You and I know the truth, and that's what matters, right?"

"What about your family?" she asked. "Your mother thinks he's yours. Are you going to tell her otherwise?"

He bit the inside of his cheek and turned to look at the house. "I haven't decided yet. I...I need some time to think about what's best."

"What's best for whom?" Larissa asked. "Because I'm pretty sure it's best for her to know whether or not she has another grandchild, and I'm *certain* it's best for you to repair any damage to your reputation."

"I need to figure out what's best for you," he clarified. "I want to do what's most protective of you and Owen. If that means allowing people to assume he's mine, then..." he trailed off, turning to stare worriedly at the house again. She knew what he was thinking as he imagined the scandal this could cause his family.

"Everett, don't," Larissa said, resting her hand on his forearm. "I'm a big girl, and I've been dealing with the situation fine on my own for seven years. Please don't bring your family into this."

"I'm not planning to," Everett said, pausing. He sighed. "I guess I want it both ways; I want to protect them and you and Owen."

"You don't owe us anything; you owe them everything. Please don't give it another thought. Tell people the truth, starting with your mother."

"Maybe," he said, still sounding doubtful. "We don't have to decide anything tonight. We'll think about it, and maybe the perfect solution will present itself." He smiled, dimpling one cheek before he took a step closer and settled his hands on her waist.

Larissa's pulse kicked into overdrive at the exact moment her mouth lost all moisture. What was he doing? Was he going to kiss her?

"You were a trooper tonight," he said. "I know it was nerve wracking to meet my family, especially with the awkward questions, but you did great. And Owen was amazing. He's such a great kid, Liss."

She beamed up at him, resting her palms uncertainly on his chest. "Thank you, Everett. And thank you for tonight. It was fun. I like your family very much."

"They like you, too. They've begun to wonder about me; I think meeting you cleared up a lot of things for them."

If only it cleared them up for her. She still wasn't sure if their exchange was friendly, or if it was leading up to a kiss. Her pulse was hammering so hard, she was sure he could feel it. There was an unknown expression on his face, the same one he'd used earlier when he told his family how they met.

"Tonight, remembering when we met, it made me realize how very much a part of me you are," Everett said. "Somehow that day our lives were woven together. I'm sorry for the years I've wasted staying away, and I'm glad that chapter is over. I'm glad we're starting again. I'm going to do it right this time, Larissa. No mistakes."

What mistakes? What was he talking about? Any mistakes in their friendship had been hers; he certainly had nothing to be ashamed of in their history together. He moved toward her and she clutched his shirt, standing on her toes, but he bypassed her lips and kissed her cheek.

"See you tomorrow, Liss," he whispered, his breath skittering across her cheek. "Sweet dreams." He stepped back and let her go, smiling as he watched her stumble to her car and drive away.

CHAPTER 13

The next morning, Detective Calhoun Boyd was waiting on Larissa when she arrived for her shift. He leaned against the bulletin board, smiling as she scanned for any new postings.

"Good morning, Officer Porter," he said.

"Good morning, Detective Boyd," Larissa said, trying to match his flirtatious tone and smile.

"You know I'm new here," he announced.

"I did notice that, but then I'm paid to be observant." Was that witty or idiotic? Larissa could only hope her smile remained placid; she was way over her head here.

His smile widened slightly as if encouraged by her banter. "I was thinking it might be nice to have someone to show me the sights."

"Of Silver Springs?" she asked, incredulous. "You could look out any window and see the entire town."

"I, ah, didn't exactly mean that literally. That was me trying to ask you out."

"Oh," Larissa said, embarrassed now and caught off guard. She thought she would have more time to work up to a date with him. Suddenly her mind was blank, and all she could think of was Everett. Would he mind if she went on a date with Cal?

Cal straightened, moving away from the bulletin board as his expression started to close. She realized then that he was taking her silence as rejection. "That sounds nice," Larissa added quickly. She rested her hand on his forearm before quickly snatching it away again, not sure if it was okay to touch him. "I need to check my schedule. It's not always easy to get a sitter for my son."

Did he know she had a son? She stood motionless, scanning his face for any signs of panic, but he nodded sympathetically. "I know what you mean. I have a little girl, but she lives with her mom. I remember how hard it was to try and find a trustworthy sitter."

"I could maybe let you know tomorrow," Larissa said, hating how uncertain she felt. Why couldn't she be good at this?

Cal's pleasant smile returned. "Sounds good. Have a good day, Officer." He tipped his head to her and she smiled.

"Thank you, Detective."

There. She did it. She accepted a date, her first since she was twelve, without making a fool of herself. At least she hoped she hadn't made a fool of herself. Cal hadn't run away screaming. That had to be a good sign, didn't it? Her relief was quickly replaced by renewed uncertainty at the thought of telling Everett. What would his reaction be?

She was distracted all day as she tried to imagine what Everett would say. How many times had he reiterated the fact that they were friends, though? At least a half dozen. Still, there was a part of her that felt jittery as she drove up the Honeywell's long lane.

Everett and Owen came out to greet her when her car came to a halt. "Hey, Liss," he said, leaning down to kiss her cheek as soon as he reached her. She smiled up at him as she hugged Owen, listening half-heartedly as her son relayed the latest farm events.

Everett's eyes narrowed as he looked her up and down. "Something wrong?"

She shook her head. "Do you want to meet us someplace tonight? I should go home and change out of my uniform."

He scanned her up and down. "You look good to me."

"Thanks, but I like to be a little less conspicuous when I go out."

He nodded. "I'll follow you home. How about if I hang on to this guy for a little bit so you can have some alone time?" He snagged Owen and put him in a loose headlock, scraping his knuckle along Owen's scalp as he tried to wriggle away.

Larissa laughed because the contact was so different than her interaction with Owen. She was thankful for Everett's presence in her son's life, and she was pretty sure her expression told him as much because he froze, blinking at her.

"That sounds nice, Everett. Thank you. Should I meet you somewhere?"

"We'll pick you up," he said. He was still looking at her, his expression so intent that it was making her stomach churn. What was he thinking when he looked at her that way?

She nodded dumbly and took a step back, connecting her hip solidly with the handle of her door.

"Okay?" Everett asked when she winced.

She nodded, still not trusting herself to speak, and made her escape before she could embarrass herself further. Why did Everett make her feel so flustered? Yes, she was in love with him and, yes, she was deeply attracted to him. Why did it sometimes seem like he felt the same?

Putting the matter from her mind, she decided to enjoy her precious free time as the rare gift it was. She hadn't taken a shower without Owen in the bathroom since his birth. At first she had been afraid to leave him alone for any length of time, strapping him in his car seat with a toy. Then, as he grew older, he had navigated to the bathroom by choice, sitting on the toilet seat to talk to her. Some of their best discussions occurred while she was in the shower, but that didn't mean she didn't enjoy the luxury of being able to have the bathroom all to herself for once.

When she arrived home, though, she felt her precious free time slipping away. Her brother, Nick stood on her front porch, and by the way he was hunched over the handle of her door, she knew he was trying to break in.

"Nick," she yelled.

He turned and looked at her, not even bothering to try and paste on a guilty expression.

"Why are you trying to break into my house?" she asked.

"I needed some money," he said, shrugging.

She prepared to give him a lecture until she drew closer and saw his face. "You're using meth," she accused. She grasped his chin between her thumb and forefinger, turning his head to the side so she could see the gaping holes his fingers had drilled into his cheeks. A side effect from coming down off meth was that it made the user feel like bugs were crawling under his skin. Lesions were a common and telling sign.

"Lay off, Larissa," Nick said, smacking her hand away. "I didn't come here for a lecture."

"I know; you came here to steal from me. Too bad for you I have nothing to steal. My electronics are outdated, and I don't keep money lying around. Call me crazy, but I know my family too well."

"If you would give me some money, I wouldn't have to take it," Nick said. His wheedling tone was already getting on her nerves, but she refrained from lecturing him again on the merits of getting a job.

"I'm not giving you money, Nick."

"But I'm *hungry*," he whined.

"Then I'll feed you. Come inside." She checked her watch, hoping she could hurry him along before Everett arrived. The two men weren't exactly on the best of terms since Nick poisoned Everett's horse and Everett had him put away for a few years in juvenile hall.

"Where's your kid?" Nick asked.

"He's with a friend," Larissa said.

Nick gave her a sharp look. "You don't have any friends, and you're never without that kid."

"I have friends," Larissa argued, though he was mostly correct. She only had one friend—Everett. She hurriedly prepared Nick a large sandwich along with an apple. He picked at the sandwich and stared suspiciously at the apple. He would leave it untouched, but she would have the satisfaction of knowing she had tried to feed him something healthy.

"Don't you have any chips or soda?" he asked.

"No," she replied. "I don't keep those things in the house. They're not healthy for Owen."

Nick laughed derisively. "He's gonna grow up to be a little wussy."

"At least he'll grow," Larissa countered. She was convinced that her small size, along with Nick's, was due to their malnourishment during childhood. When they did manage to eat, it was always cheap junk food with no nutrients.

"You know, our growing up wasn't so bad, Larissa. I don't know why you always try to make it that way."

"What did you like best about it, Nick? The neglect or the abuse?"

"Just because Mom and Dad smacked us around every once in a while to keep us in line doesn't mean it's abuse. I do the same thing to my kids when they need a pop. Your kid's probably growing up to be a spoiled brat, but it's not like I'd ever know. You don't bring him around." He shook his head before tearing off a large wad of sandwich and speaking around it. "You're such a snob, and you always have been."

"It's not Owen that keeps me away from family gatherings, Nick. I'm a police officer. How am I supposed to stand by and do nothing when I see about a hundred different laws being broken by my own family? I tried to come to Tonya's son's birthday party, but her boyfriend was in violation of his restraining order, half the family was smoking pot or drinking underage, to say nothing of the brawl that occurred before the meal even started. So, yes, pardon me if I don't want my son exposed to things he's not even allowed to watch on television."

He shook his head again. "Kid's never going to learn about real life if you keep sheltering him."

"That's not real life," Larissa said. "That's an episode of *America's Most Wanted* waiting to happen."

He actually laughed at that, and she softened slightly. "What are you doing on meth, Nicky? I thought you were smarter than that."

"Guess you were wrong," he said, sounding dismal.

"Please don't do it anymore," she said, laying her hand on his forearm. "That stuff's poison."

"Even I know that, Larissa, but it's cheap and it works like nothing else. It's too late; I'm already on the stuff, and there's no getting away from it."

"That's not true. It's never too late. There are tons of options to try and break the addiction."

"Expensive options," Nick said. "Who's going to pay for that? Welfare? Mom and Dad? You?"

"If I thought you'd really take advantage of it and make an honest effort, then, yes, I would pay for it."

"Don't waste your money." He reached up a hand to scratch his cheek, breaking open a pussy-looking scab.

Larissa pulled his hand away. "Stop picking at it. Let me put some antibacterial ointment on it before it gets infected."

"Too late," Nick said. "I have scabs on top of scabs, but I can't help it. I itch all over."

She sighed, knowing it would do no good to tell him what he already knew—that all he had to do was get off drugs and the symptoms would go away. Instead she stood and retrieved ointment from the bathroom, smearing it on his cheek with a cotton swab. As much as it hurt her to admit it, she was too afraid of what she might catch to touch the wound with her bare fingers. She knew for a fact that Nick shared needles with other users. There was no telling how many diseases he had.

"Thanks," Nick said, shifting uncomfortably when she finished. She knew that wasn't a word he used often, and she appreciated the effort it took for him to use it now. Setting aside the ointment, she put her hands on his shoulders and turned him so she could see his eyes.

"You're breaking my heart, Nick," she said. "I want better for you than this. I know you can be better, do better."

For a moment, she saw stark hope and need in his eyes, and then the front door banged open as Owen crashed inside, followed by Everett's heavy step.

"Mommy, we're home," Owen called.

"Liss, you ready?" Everett added.

Nick's expression became guarded again and then openly hostile as Everett walked into the kitchen. "What's he doing here?" Nick asked, jerking free of Larissa's touch.

"He's a friend," Larissa said. She hoped her soft and gentle tone would work to tamp down her brother's rising temper, but no such luck. He stood so abruptly that the ladder-back chair he had been sitting on toppled to the floor.

"I don't believe this," Nick said. "You're friends with a *Honeywell?*" He tore his eyes off Everett to turn them accusingly on Larissa.

"Yes, I am," Larissa said evenly, noting in her peripheral vision that Owen crept slightly closer to Everett for protection. He had seen Nick in a rage a couple of times before, and, though he had been much younger, he must have remembered.

"They sent me to jail, Larissa," Nick said, punctuating each word with a stiff finger jab to Larissa's chest. Everett took a step forward, but Larissa held up her hand to hold him off.

"You sent yourself to jail when you poisoned their horse, Nick," Larissa said. "The Honeywells didn't attack you; you attacked *them.*"

"I didn't do it," Nick said. "I was set up. They probably did it for the insurance money, and I was an easy patsy."

She knew it wasn't so because she'd heard him confess, but he didn't know that she'd heard. To this day he had no idea that she was the secret witness who turned him in and swore out a sealed statement to the sheriff. "You're lying and you know it," Larissa said. "Your anger at the Honeywells is misplaced. They've been nothing but kind to me and Owen, and I won't have you talking badly about them in my house."

When he swung at her, she was prepared, and so was Everett. She ducked out of the way, dodging easily to the side to escape the blow. Nick's first response to anything was always violence, and he always led with a right hook. Everett, who had probably been waiting impatiently for his chance to join the fray, picked Nick up and pinned his legs and arms behind his back like an errant calf. Everett was so tall and Nick was so small that it was as easy as lifting a child. In fact, he was probably using restraint to make sure he didn't do any permanent damage.

"Time to say goodbye to your sister," Everett said, though who knows if Nick heard him over his own invectives. He was hurling epithets at Everett, Larissa, and life in general as Larissa shifted closer to Owen and put her hands over his ears.

Everett returned a few minutes later and, miraculously, all traces of Nick were gone. Usually he was much more persistent when he was angry, but whatever Everett said to him must have worked to send him away for the evening.

"You okay?" he asked Larissa as soon as he rejoined the kitchen.

She nodded, giving him a reassuring smile. "Same old, same old," she said. She glanced down at Owen who was still standing frozen beneath her hands. Everett reached out and ruffled his hair, smiling.

"That was a lot of excitement, huh?" Everett asked him.

Owen nodded. "You picked him up and carried him out," he said, sounding awed.

"Sure I did," Everett said. "We have to protect your mom, don't we?"

"But I can't do that," Owen said. "I'm too little. And…and Uncle Nick scares me."

"Some day you'll be able to protect her like that. You're going to be tall and strong. But for now, maybe you can leave it to me until you're able to take over, okay?"

Owen nodded. Larissa felt the need to jump in and say she could take care of herself. After all, she had perfected the art of dodging blows or learning how to take them and keep going, but Owen and Everett seemed to be having some sort of guy moment that she didn't understand, and she was loathe to intrude.

"Honey, Uncle Nick is not going to hurt me," she said instead.

"No, he's not," Everett agreed. His grave tone let her know that she was once again under his complete protection. Instead of feeling reassured, however, she felt stifled. Though she appreciated the sentiment, she was a grown woman and a cop. She could take care of herself, especially where her own brother was concerned.

"Why don't we stay in tonight and get pizza instead?" Everett suggested.

Owen sagged slightly in relief, making Larissa wonder if he had been afraid to go out, afraid they would run into Nick again. "That sounds nice," Larissa agreed. "Why don't you go wash up, Owen?"

"Mom, I already washed my hands at the Honeywells," Owen complained.

"You know I like you to wash before we eat," Larissa said. He opened his mouth to protest again, but she gave him "the look," the one that said if he argued again, he was going to get it. He frowned, but he turned and plodded toward the bathroom.

"Are you really okay?" Everett said, stepping forward to close the distance between them as soon as Owen left the room.

"I really am," Larissa said.

"Does this sort of thing happen often?"

"Only whenever I see him, which isn't very often," she said.

"I don't like that, Lissy. I don't like that you're in danger so often."

"Everett, I'm a police officer. I'm in danger every day."

"Yes, but this is Silver Springs." He waved his hand dismissively toward the town.

She smiled, shaking her head. "You have no idea what goes on behind closed doors, but I do. Believe me when I tell you my family isn't alone in their outrageous behavior. Some people are better at hiding it. I've been in some hair-raising situations, but I can handle myself."

Everett was frowning now with much the same expression that Owen had used. "I don't like that, Liss."

"That's my job and Nick's my family. Neither is going to change any time soon." She reached out and squeezed his bicep. "Don't look so worried, Everett. I'm fine."

"But I am worried," he said. His hand rested lightly on her shoulder before skimming down to her elbow and back up again. It was an innocent touch, but Larissa felt it all the way to her marrow. "I keep thinking about all the wasted years you were alone, and I could kick myself. Maybe if I hadn't left you to fend for yourself, then you wouldn't have become a cop. Maybe your brother would know better than to try and take a swing at you every time he's angry."

"Everett, please stop," Larissa said. Unconsciously, her palm rested on his stomach. "How many times do I have to tell you that I'm not your responsibility? Good or bad, my life is my own."

He was frowning harder now. "But you are. Don't you understand that, Larissa? You're my responsibility not because you have to be but because I want you to be. This is what friends do; they take care of each other."

"How do I take care of you?" She whispered the question that had been on her mind for years. What did Everett get from their friendship except a whole lot of hassle? The quick rush of words brought her another step closer and she laid her other palm on his stomach. They were very close together now. He gripped her other elbow and, if she were taller, they would have been nose to nose.

"Are you guys going to kiss?" Owen stopped short in the doorway, staring at Everett and Larissa with wide eyes.

Everett dropped his arms and backed away. "Of course not, bud," he said, smiling. "Your mom and I are friends. Friends don't kiss."

"Okay," Owen said. He sounded as uncertain as Larissa felt because if she had come upon the intimate little scene between her and Everett, she would have assumed the same thing. If they hadn't been about to kiss, then why did it feel like they had? Was she really so bad at reading signals?

"Why don't you go take your shower now and Owen and I will order the pizza," Everett suggested.

"All right," Larissa said, preparing to salvage as much of the evening as she could. She would be cheerful for Owen's sake, but she didn't have to force it much. Maybe she should be more abashed that her sibling had tried to deck her, but it was pretty much par for the course for their family. She was far more encouraged over the conversation they'd shared before than she was upset over the argument.

The pizza had arrived by the time Larissa exited the bathroom. Her hair was still wet, and she left it hanging long down her back. She stood on her toes to reach the plates. Everett stood over her and pulled them down, pausing to lean over her and sniff.

"You smell great," he said, smiling.

"Thank you," she said, feeling off kilter by his nearness. "You, too," she added, and he did. He smelled as good as he looked, which was saying something because he looked amazing. Even though he was almost seven feet tall, he was well proportioned for his size. Unlike some tall men who looked as if they were a piece of rubber that had been stretched to the breaking point, Everett's shoulders were wide and his frame solid. He was well muscled without being overly large. In short, he was perfect. Larissa realized she was staring and snapped to attention, setting the plates on the table. Her thoughts turned to Calhoun Boyd, and she felt disloyal, though she wasn't sure who she owed her loyalty to—the man with whom she had a date tomorrow, or Everett who insisted they were friends.

Owen kept up a lively discussion over supper, sparing Larissa from having to talk. Everett listened to Owen with a smile, glancing occasionally at Larissa over the top of his head. The scene was like something from Larissa's wildest fantasies—mom, dad, and child, discussing their day over supper. But Everett wasn't the dad in this scenario, and she couldn't forget that. As much as she thought he was her ideal, he had no desire to be a part of their family in any real way.

Dusk was firmly in place, but after supper Everett and Owen still went outside and tossed the football for a while as Larissa sat on the porch and watched with a smile. What would Owen think of Calhoun? Not that she had any intention of introducing him at this stage. She wouldn't introduce Owen to a man until things became serious. How had Everett bypassed that rule? Somehow he had sneaked behind the perimeter she had set in place since Owen's birth. Now, seeing how firmly and easily Owen had attached himself to Everett, Larissa was glad for the rule. She wouldn't want him latching on to anyone this way. She realized then how much she trusted Everett. He wouldn't drop Owen. He would stick around and be a part of his life, the same way he had been a part of her life for so many years.

"Catch, Lissy," Everett said, tossing her the ball. She caught it, pulling it tight into her chest. "Good job," Everett added.

"Mom's pretty good at playing ball—for a girl," Owen said.

"For a girl?" Larissa said. "Who says girls can't be good at ball?"

"Everyone knows guys are better at sports, Mom," Owen said. She couldn't see him in the semi-darkness, but it was a safe bet he was rolling his eyes.

"There are lots of female athletes who are as good as men, Owen," Larissa said, trying to tamp down her frustration. No matter how hard she tried to show him that women were as capable as men, it was as if misogyny was built into his DNA.

"Tell her I'm right, Everett," Owen said.

"I wouldn't presume to disagree with your mom on this one, bud," Everett said. "And there are some things that women are even better at than men."

"Like what?" Owen asked.

"Like looking pretty and smelling good," Everett said. "Your mom's the best at that one." He tossed the ball to Larissa again while Owen studied her, trying to determine if what Everett had said was true.

"Yeah, I guess you're right," Owen said. "Mom's pretty. I've seen some of my friends' moms, and they're old. Some of them are fat."

"Owen!" Larissa exclaimed. "That's not nice."

"It's nice to *you*," Owen said, and Everett laughed.

"Still," Larissa said. "It's not nice to call people fat."

"But they are fat, Mom. I'm stating a point."

Everett laughed again. Larissa shot him a look that was probably lost in the darkness, but he must have felt the effects because he stopped laughing and cleared his throat.

"It's time for a bath," Larissa said to Owen.

"Aw, Mom," he said. "I took a bath last night."

Larissa didn't argue; she simply caught the football and turned to go inside. Everett followed, and Owen brought up the rear. "Are you staying?" she asked. "I need to talk to you."

"Okay," Everett said. His casual tone told her he had already been intending to stay. She hurried through Owen's bath and nighttime routine, feeling unaccountably nervous about the upcoming conversation with Everett. Despite his insistence that they were nothing but friends, Larissa was concerned about his reaction to the information that she had a date with another man. Maybe she was wrong, but she thought he had some attraction to her, even if he didn't realize it.

"Everything go okay?" Everett asked when she returned to the living room. "I didn't hear any screaming."

"It went okay," she said. "He usually goes down pretty well. The complaining is new. I think he's testing his limits." She sat beside him on the couch.

He smiled, turning toward her to tuck a strand of hair behind her ear. "What did you want to talk to me about?"

"I don't quite know how to begin, so I guess I'll blurt it out. I have a date."

For a split second he stared at her as something she didn't understand flashed across his face. And then it was gone, replaced by his usually placid smile. "With who?"

"You don't know him. He's new to the area—Detective Calhoun Boyd."

"Sounds nice."

"So you don't mind?" she asked.

"Mind? Why would I mind? We're friends. You're free to date anyone you want. In fact, I can watch Owen for you if you don't have a sitter."

"That would be great," she said, trying to tamp down her disappointment. What had she expected? That Everett would declare his undying love for her and forbid her from seeing another man? Fat chance.

He picked up the remote and turned to a game. They watched in silence for a while until Larissa yawned. "I should let you go." He set the remote on the table and turned to give her his standard goodbye kiss on the cheek, only he didn't. Instead he bypassed her cheek and kissed her lips.

CHAPTER 14

$\mathcal{E}$verett sat in his car, gripping the steering wheel. He should go. He should drive away and remove himself from the temptation of going back inside and finishing what he started with Larissa.

Why had he kissed her? At least he had somehow kept it as a soft and gentle kiss, belying none of the roaring emotion and attraction he felt for her. He took a deep breath, held it, and let it out slowly. Somehow when he hatched his plan to win her back, he never imagined another man in the scenario. What was he supposed to do now when every instinct was telling him to go back inside, tell her how he felt, and kiss her again?

His hands clenched on the steering wheel, trying to anchor himself in place. He couldn't go back; he couldn't forgo the plan. He was doing things right this time, not like seven years ago when he'd made a disaster of everything.

If only he hadn't kissed her that night seven years ago. If he hadn't kissed her, then he wouldn't have left before finding out that her ride had gone. He would have taken her home, and she would have been safe. Then, sometime down the road when she was out of school, things might have been different for them.

But that hadn't happened. Everett had given in to temptation and kissed her. Not kissed her but *kissed* her, with a capital K, the kind of kiss he would be embarrassed for anyone to know had occurred with someone his own age, let alone a sixteen year old at a party. And then he had left her there at the mercy of someone who had taken advantage of her innocence.

As if all that wasn't enough, he had recently learned of another glaring failure when he allowed his hurt and confusion to leave her in the hospital all those years ago. He had gone with the best of intentions, feeling very superior about himself. After all, the first time he saw her around town in her very pregnant state, he nearly fell over himself in an effort to get away from her. He had retreated to the safety of his car, glad for the black tinting on the windows.

For a moment, his shock made him confused. Judging by the size of her, she had been about five months along and it had been five months since the party. Did they…Had they…No, he had run away. That much he had remembered. The baby wasn't his; that was ridiculous. But if not his, then whose? To his knowledge, she wasn't dating anyone. His first ugly thought was that someone in her family had taken advantage of her—her brother, maybe. He was the type whose depravity knew no bounds, but then Everett remembered that Nick was still in juvenile hall. Whose baby was she carrying?

The thought tormented him, keeping him up nights, keeping him away from her. He was afraid if he saw her, she would read what was in his heart and in his eyes—the disappointment that she had turned out exactly like people thought she would combined with the disappointment that the child in question wasn't his.

Up until that night, until he kissed Larissa, he had never known what it was to truly want something he couldn't have. Kissing her, even in the most innocent way, was wrong, but Everett had done way more than that. And he wanted to do more. He had sat in his SUV that first day he saw her pregnant and called himself every kind of name. How could he judge her brother for being depraved when he had somehow fallen in love with a child? And not any child, but one who had been under his protection for almost all her life? Maybe he needed therapy. Maybe he needed a girlfriend. But the thought of dating anyone else, of kissing anyone but Larissa, was repugnant to him.

For the next few months, he stewed in his misery, waiting for the father to step forward and do the right thing by her. But when none appeared, Everett took matters into his own hands. He waited until she was in the hospital and then he went to see her, intending to find out the truth, once and for all.

Haltingly, Larissa had told him the truth, her face crimson and averted as if she were the one who had a right to feel ashamed. White hot rage sliced through Everett's midsection as he heard her tale, both at her attacker and at himself. He was almost as much to blame as the man who had put her in this condition. How could he have left her alone at that party? It was his own weakness that had hurt her. Once again Larissa was a hapless victim of circumstance, only now it was in the cruelest way. No one would ever believe a Porter hadn't gotten pregnant the old fashioned way—by consent. Larissa--who had tried so hard to be good, to live above her family's reputation--was now sullied by *his* action. Everett swore to make it right, but what could he do?

The nurse had brought her baby in then. Everett hadn't wanted to look at him, hadn't wanted to know what his failure had brought about, but he couldn't help himself. As Larissa's face lit with the radiance of love, Everett had to see what was bringing her such joy. And when he looked, he gasped out loud; it was like looking at a miniature of himself.

Larissa had glanced over her son's head, locking eyes with him, knowing what he was thinking. "He looked like you, the man." And for the first time since he arrived at the hospital, she burst into tears, so loud and so convulsive that Everett reached out to take baby Owen from her, holding the fragile infant with one arm as he held Larissa with the other. For a too brief moment, she had molded herself to him, pressing her face to his chest and surrendering to her tears. His heart had shattered and broken into a million tiny pieces that day and he swore to do whatever it took to make things right again, both with

Larissa and with himself. He opened his mouth to tell her as much when she shrugged from his embrace and sat back.

"Go, Everett, please go. This is a terrible mess, and I don't want you involved."

"You want me to go?" Everett had asked as he unconsciously swayed the infant in his arms.

Larissa had nodded, not quite meeting his eyes. "I can't be friends with you anymore. I have my son to think about now."

At the time, Everett hadn't understood. He had handed Owen back to her, stood, and walked from the room. Pausing in the doorway, he had looked at the beautiful picture Larissa made as she bent over her tiny son. Leaving felt wrong, but Everett was hurt. She didn't want him in her life. He had hurt her too much. This mess was his fault, and she knew it. Slowly, he had walked from the room, feeling with every step as if he were leaving a piece of himself behind.

The problem, he realized now as he sat in his car, was that he had no idea what to do. Seven years later, and he hadn't developed a plan to undo his horrendous mistake. He felt almost paralyzed by fear—stuck in neutral. His brothers, Brent, Corliss, and Darcy, all made it look so easy. But relating to the opposite sex had never come easily for Everett. Most women were intimidated either by his size or his silence. He had learned it was better to keep his distance than to risk scaring a woman or having his heart broken. Staying away from Larissa had never been an option, though. She needed him, now as much as ever, she just didn't see it.

This time around he would do things right. He would build on their friendship until it was strong enough to slowly advance to romance. That had been his strategy since the day Larissa arrested Grant, but now with the thought of another man coming between them, Everett felt an almost desperate need to sprint back to her and claim what was his. He sat gripping the steering wheel, white knuck-led, until his panic ebbed. He wouldn't go back. He would stick with his plan, do things the right way, and work on their friendship. Surely one date couldn't hurt anything, could it?

CHAPTER 15

Calhoun Boyd cleaned up well. Technically he was dressed down from the usual shirt and tie he wore for work, but he looked good in jeans and a cotton knit shirt that conformed to his well-built physique. His manners were impeccable, and the date was going well. Why, then, couldn't Larissa stop thinking about Everett?

He had shown up early to take care of Owen, keeping him occupied while Larissa finished getting ready. She had changed outfits three times and spent longer than normal on her hair and makeup until she was finally satisfied, and even then she had stood staring uncertainly at herself in the mirror. What was she doing? Was she ready for this? Why had going on a date seemed like a good idea? What did she really know about Calhoun Boyd? What did she know about dating?

Before panic could overwhelm and paralyze her, she made herself step away from the mirror and exit the bathroom. Everett and Owen were in the living room, Owen's baseball cards spread on the floor between them.

"I'm missing one," Owen announced. "I'm going to go look under my bed." He skittered to his bedroom, ignoring Larissa as if she were a piece of furniture. When she realized she had been counting on a word of encouragement from her seven-year-old son, she felt more than a little pathetic.

Everett looked up at her and stood, smiling down at her in approval. "Nervous?" he asked.

"A little. I haven't been on a date since I was twelve, and you know how that one ended."

"This one can end the same way if he gives you any trouble. Call me if you need me, Liss, and I'll come get you."

She smiled at his suddenly fierce expression. "Everett, when are you going to realize I'm not a kid anymore?"

"I realize," he said.

Her heart flipped over. How did he manage to make his tone so intent and his expression so light? He confused her. "Thanks for watching Owen for me," she whispered.

"What are friends for?" he asked, and then they stood there, staring at each other. He reached down and tucked a strand of hair behind her ear. "You're beautiful."

You're beautiful, not *you* look *beautiful.* The difference in statements wasn't lost on Larissa. "Thank you," she said. "I'm always thanking you for something, Everett. Did you ever notice that? You do so much for me, and in return, I…"

He picked her up, stopping her speech mid-sentence as she blinked at him in surprise. His arms were wrapped around her waist, doubled over so that she was cinched tight against his chest. "Stop, Liss. Friends don't keep a balance sheet, especially not when we've been friends as long as you and I have."

She wanted to argue with him, but she couldn't think of a thing to say as she dangled there, helplessly suspended in his arms. She hadn't been this close to him since they kissed seven years ago. He had lifted her like this then, pinning her against the wall while he kissed her senseless. It was difficult not to remember, especially with the kiss from last night fresh in her head. Of course, last night's kiss had been a friendly peck, nothing like the one they'd shared on the fateful night that changed her life. Did he still think about their first kiss? Had it embedded itself into his head the way it had dug into hers? Of course not. He was Everett, the self-avowed eternal bachelor.

"Why have you never dated, Everett?" Larissa asked. "You have so much to offer."

"I'm glad you think so," he said, ignoring her question.

Suddenly, however, it was vitally important to Larissa that he answer. Did he really not want to marry anyone, to date? "Why? Why don't you go out with anyone? Even if you don't want to get serious, you could go out once in a while." She broke off as a new thought occurred to her. "Or do you? I guess we've never really said. Maybe you have a girlfriend." She let the thought hang, waiting for him to deny it, but he smiled. He was very good at remaining mute, keeping everything bottled inside to keep people guessing. Larissa didn't want to guess about him, though. She wanted to know exactly what was going on with him.

Before she could press the issue, Cal knocked on the door, effectively ending the discussion. Everett set her down and gave her biceps a squeeze. "Remember what I said; if you're uncomfortable, or afraid, or even bored, you can call me and I'll come get you. No matter what."

Larissa forced a smile, trying not to be hurt at the fact that Everett still hadn't answered her question about his dating habits. "I'll be fine, Everett. I left instructions for Owen on the kitchen table. He's already had his bath, so you'll have to read him a couple of stories before bed. Don't let him try to talk you into staying up late. His bedtime is eight."

"You won't be back before then?" Everett asked.

Larissa laughed. "That's only two hours away. I'm pretty sure the date's going to last longer than that."

But now that it was eight, Larissa was ready for the date to be over. Not for the first time she wondered what was wrong with her. Here she was with Cal who made no secret of his desire to be more than friends, but all she could think about was Everett who made no secret of his desire to be friends. Her nerves had died away after the first few minutes with Calhoun, as soon as she realized they would never be more than friends. He was handsome and funny, but the attraction wasn't there, at least not on her end. Once she realized things were going to be platonic between them, she had relaxed. She was having fun, but there was a part of her that wanted to be with Owen, tucking him into bed and kissing him goodnight. This was the first time she had ever not been the one to put him to bed, but it was more than that. She wanted to be with Everett.

Somehow she had become used to the routine of putting Owen to bed and meeting up with Everett on the couch. Sitting beside him and watching television in comfortable silence had become the best part of her day, something she looked forward to. Now she and Cal were sitting side by side at a movie and she had no idea that he was going to reach for her hand until it happened. It was a friendly clasp, but she still felt like she was betraying Everett somehow. That was crazy, though, since they were nothing more than friends. In fact, Everett had done everything but shove her out the door when Cal arrived, retreating to Owen's room so she could greet her date in private.

Larissa found his thoughtfulness painful. Why couldn't he make a jealous scene, hover protectively behind her, and put his seal on her so firmly that Cal would run away with his tail tucked between his legs? She was hopeless; the situation was hopeless. She might as well learn to like Cal and give up on wanting anything more from Everett than he was willing to offer. Maybe in time she would learn to like Cal as more than a friend. Maybe she would stop picturing Everett every time she looked at Cal.

After the movie they grabbed coffee and talked. Larissa learned Cal had only been divorced a year, and she was his first date since his separation. From the way he talked about his wife and daughter, Larissa knew he missed them like crazy. She didn't know him well enough to say so, but it was her opinion that he was still in love with his wife.

"Is she remarried?" she asked.

"I think she dates occasionally," he said. The way his hand clenched on his coffee mug told her the thought of his wife with another man was eating him alive with jealousy.

"Why did you get divorced?" she asked. It was a nosy question, but if neither of them was seeing anyone else, she didn't understand why things hadn't worked out.

Cal took a breath and released it slowly. "I wish I could point to one thing and say 'This is why,' but it's not like that. I was working a lot, the baby brought a lot of pressure, Sarah was unhappy with life in general, and we started fighting all the time. Getting a divorce seemed like the best solution."

When was getting a divorce ever the best solution? "But if you love her, why not stay and work things out?"

It wasn't her imagination that his smile was patronizing. "You're young, and you've never been married. Sometimes what makes rational sense doesn't translate emotionally, and vice versa. Sarah and I were high school sweethearts. I never thought we would end up divorced, but sometimes it's like things happen that are outside your control or plan. I don't know how to explain it, but it was like we had to get away from each other, like that was going to fix everything."

Only it hadn't. Larissa could tell by the resigned way he spoke. How sad to have found love, only to lose it. If she were ever lucky enough to love and be loved in return, there wouldn't be anything that could make her give it up. They talked for a long time or, rather, Cal talked and Larissa listened. Not that she minded. It was sort of nice to be there for someone, to be a caring friend and listening ear for someone who needed one.

Larissa thought they were on the same page, so she was taken by surprise when Cal kissed her goodnight. She thought he was walking her to her front door to be polite, but then he leaned down and kissed her. For a few seconds, she was frozen, unable to think of a word to say.

"Thank you," she said at last.

Cal laughed. "That's the first time anyone had ever thanked me for kissing her. I had fun tonight, Larissa. I hope we can do this again sometime."

Larissa nodded. "Sure," she said, feeling more confused than ever. She would like to be friends with him, and go out as such, but was that what he meant? How did people navigate the dating world? It was all a mystery to her. Cal stood back and watched as she opened her door and let herself inside. She wondered if he was waiting for an invitation to come in, but there was no way she was doing that. She had somehow managed to go the whole evening without mentioning who was watching Owen, but it would be awkward to try and explain Everett's presence in her living room.

She closed the door and leaned against it, still feeling muddled from the goodnight kiss. Everett didn't turn around to look at her, and she wondered if he had heard her come in. He was watching the evening news, and it must have been mesmerizing.

"Hi," Larissa said, but he didn't turn around. She left the safety of the door and walked toward him. "How did it go with Owen?"

"Fine," Everett said. He snapped off the television, but still didn't look at her. Tentatively, she sat beside him, studying his profile for some clue to his behavior.

"Everything okay?" she asked.

He turned toward her then, his mouth open to answer. Then his jaw snapped shut and he shook his head. "I can't do this," he said.

Before she could ask him what he meant, he stood and let himself out the door, closing it firmly in his wake.

The next day was Sunday, Larissa's day off. She sat at the kitchen table, sipping her coffee and puzzling over the previous evening when Owen piped up from the opposite side of the table.

"Are we going to see Everett today?"

"I don't know," Larissa said. "He didn't mention anything. Did he say anything last night?" Was it wrong to pump her child for information?

"No." Owen paused, chewing. "He seemed sort of sad last night. He asked a bunch of questions about you."

"Like what?" Larissa sipped her coffee, keeping her eyes carefully on the table.

"I don't know. Stuff. What are we going to do today? Can we go to the Honeywell's so I can visit the new foal?"

"I don't think so, honey, but you'll be there tomorrow. Let's spend some Mom and Owen time today."

"But I want to see Everett," Owen said, pouting.

"Owen, we survived without Everett for seven years. We can survive one day." She said it as much to herself as to him. The day suddenly stretched out long and lonely before her. "Want to go for a hike?"

"Can we invite Everett?" Owen asked, perking up considerably.

"Okay," Larissa said before she could talk herself out of it. She reached for her phone and called, noting that she had somehow already memorized his phone number, but it went to voicemail. "Everett, Owen and I were going hiking, and I wondered if you wanted to join us." She paused, wanting to add more, but not knowing what to say. She turned away from Owen and lowered her voice. "I was hoping to talk to you about last night. I'm sorry about whatever happened." She closed the phone, staring at it and willing for him to call her back, but he didn't.

She and Owen went hiking on their own, trying not to feel like something was missing. Larissa surreptitiously checked her voicemail throughout the day, but Everett never called. Why was he so angry?

The next morning, Monday, Cal was waiting for her again near the briefing board. "Hey, we didn't really talk about how we were going to handle things at work."

What things? We've had one date. "Um, I guess we'll play it cool."

He nodded. "That's what I was thinking, too. So, what do you think about a redo next weekend?"

"Can I let you know? I'm not sure about a sitter for Owen."

"Can't you use the same one you used this weekend?" he asked.

"I don't know if that's going to work out again," Larissa said, her mind flashing to Everett and his obvious anger and rejection.

"Fingers crossed something works out," Cal said.

"Fingers crossed," Larissa added.

He smiled. "Have a good day today."

"You, too," she said, smiling lamely as he walked away.

Because things had been so quiet lately, Larissa assumed she would have a good day, which was her first mistake. Her second was not waiting for backup when the domestic call came. Domestic situations during a weekday afternoon were unusual to begin with. On a normal day, at least one half of a couple was at work, and it was generally too early for anyone to be drunk. There were always exceptions, however, and this was one of those times.

The call was placed by a concerned neighbor who heard loud arguing coming from the residence. There was no previous call history at the house which meant that either the couple in question was new or they had been keeping things under wraps. Larissa had learned not to be surprised by the things people could keep secret. The third option was that it was simply a screaming match and a word of warning would be enough to quiet them down. Larissa hoped it was that one because her backup, an older officer named Henry who was on the verge of retirement, was across town serving a civil paper.

When she approached the porch, however, her hopes for a peaceful resolution evaporated. Through the door, she saw a man. His back was to her as he pummeled whoever was unfortunate enough to be beneath him. From the screams, Larissa guessed it was a woman.

She quickly radioed the situation to her dispatch and requested backup, then opened the door and stepped inside, shouting for the man to stop. He paid her no mind as his meaty fists brutally pounded into the woman on the floor. By now her face was a mess of bloody pulp. Larissa knew if she didn't stop him, the woman would soon be dead. She tackled the man, knocking him backwards to the ground.

"Get out of here," she managed to say to the woman, and then the man turned his fury on Larissa. She was prepared for him and had no intentions of being a helpless victim. They rolled over and over, knocking into furniture as they struggled for supremacy. Larissa knew that if she allowed him to pin her, she would end up like the poor woman who was now crawling away on her hands and knees.

The man was huge, and he was angry, but he didn't really know how to fight. His menacing size had probably always been enough of an advantage before, but Larissa had spent years learning how to duck and take a blow—first through her abusive childhood, and then from her training at the police academy. That training and experience gave her the advantage she needed to keep from being a docile punching bag. Not that he wasn't getting his licks in, because he was. But Larissa was giving as good as she got and also protecting her head and face. Still, his fists slammed into her body over and over again as they struggled back and forth.

At one point when they rolled, her ankle was pinned beneath him. There was a horrible popping sound and searing pain. In fact, everything hurt. The key was to not give in to the pain. If she did, if she stopped to ponder any of the injuries she was receiving, she was toast.

At last the pain began to overtake her survival instinct. If she didn't end this now, then there was a good chance he could kill her. Somehow, she managed to get in a few jabs to his kidneys, incapacitating him enough so that she could bring her knee up between his legs hard enough to stun him even further. She sprung into action then, knowing he wouldn't be out of it for long. Rolling him onto his stomach, she wrenched his arms behind his back and cuffed him, panting through her own pain and misery.

He heaved a couple of times, but didn't throw up. Larissa felt like doing the same thing. The pain was intense, and she couldn't tell what hurt the most—her sides or her ankle.

Outside a car door slammed, and she sagged slightly in relief. Backup was here. It was almost over. She turned toward the door as Henry stepped through, weapon drawn. Then the suspect beneath her reared back, slamming his skull hard against her temple so that everything faded to black.

When Larissa woke, her eyes felt heavy. It was an unnatural kind of heaviness, the kind induced by painkillers, though not all the pain was gone. Her head throbbed, as did her ankle, and there was a sharp stab of pain in her sides every time she breathed. The only pleasantness at this moment was the warm softness nestled against her neck. Was it Owen? Was he burrowed against her, seeking comfort?

Instinctively, she rested her hand comfortingly on the head, fitting her fingers into the thick thatch of hair. This noggin, however, was much larger than Owen's.

"Liss."

The whispered nickname was only used by one person, but Larissa still cracked one eyelid to be sure. She met the obsidian gaze of Everett whose face was hovering a centimeter away, his breath warm on her neck.

"I was listening to your pulse," he explained. "You've been out so long. I wanted to reassure myself you're okay. I'm sorry I woke you."

"It's okay," she tried to reassure him, but her mouth was so dry the words wouldn't form.

Everett, guessing the problem, reached for a cup from the stand

and held a straw to her lips. "They gave you morphine. It dries everything out."

"What's wrong with me?" she asked after a few satisfying sips of water.

"Sprained ankle, a few broken ribs, and probably a killer headache from being knocked out."

She started to nod, but stopped short when it hurt too much. Instead, she simply closed her eyes and rested her head on the pillow.

"Can I get you anything else?" One of his hands clasped hers. The other smoothed gently over her forehead in the same motion Larissa used on Owen whenever he was ill.

Her eyes flew open as she remembered her son. "Owen."

"He's fine," Everett assured her. "He's in the lobby with my parents."

"Oh," she said, relaxing against the bed again. "How did you know about this?"

"Owen called me. One of your coworkers showed up at school to pick him up, but Owen had never met him, and he wasn't on the approved pickup list. Owen was scared and upset. He told them I was his dad, and they called me."

When Larissa winced, it wasn't from pain; it was from mortification. Owen had told the school that Everett was his dad. She wasn't naïve enough to think that sort of bombshell information would stay under wraps, especially not when everyone in town knew who the Honeywells were.

"Who was the friend from work?" Larissa asked, dreading the answer.

"Calhoun Boyd," Everett said. "He stayed around until I showed up. It was awkward. You probably have a lot of explaining to do. I'm sorry about that." He didn't sound sorry, though. He sounded remarkably cheerful for someone who had become a very big source of gossip. "And I'm sorry I left on Saturday and didn't call Sunday. I didn't handle that very well."

Handle what well? Before she could ask, he kept speaking.

"Also, I lied."

That certainly caught her attention. As far as she knew, Everett had never lied in his life. "You lied?"

He nodded, looking very serious now. "When Owen, my parents, and I arrived, they wouldn't let me see you or tell me anything. Everyone was being so cryptic and secretive; I was going insane. So I told them we're engaged."

Larissa drew in a quick breath and winced again, this time from the pain in her ribs. "Everett, you never lie. You hate lying."

"Turns out what I hate even more is being scared out of my mind that you're dying and not being able to reassure Owen that you're going to be okay. It seemed like the only solution at the time."

"Did your parents hear?"

"Everyone heard, Liss. I sort of yelled it. Between the hospital and the school, we're about to become very big news." Larissa groaned and he clutched her hand tighter. "I'm sorry," he added.

She gave a half-hearted laugh at that. "Why are you apologizing? I'm the one who's sorry. You were trying to protect Owen, and now you're all tangled up in this mess. You're innocent, but now no one will ever believe you're not Owen's dad."

"You're innocent, too," he said. "And so is Owen."

"But this is still all my fault." She placed her hand over her eyes to fight the sudden rush of tears. When people had finally stopped talking about her, had finally stopped trying to solve the mystery of Owen's father, why did this have to happen? And to Everett, no less. Larissa had always feared that he would come to regret his friendship with her. Now that day had arrived.

"You must rue the day you sat on that step and wiped my tears, Everett. What a mess." Her voice broke on the last word, and she swiped at her eyes.

"That's not even a little bit true, Larissa. Don't even joke about something like that," Everett said. He caught her hand and pulled it away from her face so she had no choice but to look at his fierce, earnest expression. "How could you think even for a moment that I regret anything to do with you? If I regret anything, it's those seven wasted years you were alone. I should have married you when you were sixteen."

The shock of that statement was enough to dry her tears. Had that thought actually been a possibility? How could he think his life would have been better by adding a teenage bride and a child who wasn't his? That was Everett, though, always thinking about what was best for her. If only she could do the same for him for once.

"I wish I could fix this," she said.

"Maybe you can," Everett said. He shifted his gaze so that he was looking at their clasped hands instead of at her face. "You could marry me now."

What? What had he said? Because surely he hadn't said what she thought he said; that was crazy. He couldn't still think marriage was the best option, could he? Until recently, they hadn't spoken in seven years. She had only kissed him once; they'd never had a date. "What?" she said after a lengthy and uncomfortable silence.

He gripped her hand tighter, looking into her eyes once again. "Think about it, Liss. You're right; people will never believe I'm not Owen's dad now. No one will understand why I won't marry the mother of my child, especially since we're going to be spending so much time together. But if we get married, the talk will go away. What's the worst they can say? That it took me long enough to do the right thing? That's not so bad; we can handle that."

"Everett, marriage isn't a solution to a problem. It's huge; it's monumental."

"But we already know we're compatible. We've been friends for seventeen years. Owen approves. I have a steady job and no money worries. What are we missing?"

Love, she thought. She wanted Everett to love her the way a husband loves his wife. She wanted him to say they had to get married because he couldn't live without her, because he was crazy about her.

"What happened to Mr. I'm-never-getting-married?" she asked.

"Desperate times and all that. Besides, it's not like I'm marrying some stranger off the street. I know what to expect with you."

She wasn't sure what that meant, but it didn't sound very romantic.

She wanted him to be so head over heels in love that he couldn't think of one rational reason their marriage shouldn't work. Instead he had made a list of some very rational reasons it would be a great idea. She still planned on saying no, though. She couldn't marry him. It was crazy. She opened her mouth to tell him so when his mother's face popped into her head. It was the visage of the stately Mrs. Honeywell that changed Larissa's mind. The woman was so respectable and above reproach. She didn't deserve to have her family name dragged through the mud like a common Porter. If there was one thing Larissa could do to prevent that, she would do it—not only for Everett, but for all the Honeywells.

"All right, Everett. I'll marry you."

Everett surprised her again by beaming as if she'd handed him a prize-winning stallion. "We'll be happy, Liss. I know it." He crept closer, gingerly wrapping her in his arms while trying not to jostle her.

At least now he'll have to kiss me, Larissa thought as her heartbeat kicked into overdrive. She rubbed her cheek gently against his, noting as she did so the way his stubble scraped her tender skin. The atmosphere in the room suddenly felt tense as Everett eased away from her slightly, his gaze dropping to her lips.

He inched closer, and Larissa tipped her head back, ignoring the pain, wanting nothing more than to kiss this man and be kissed in return.

"Mommy."

They froze as Owen's anxious voice echoed around the room. Thankfully he had been so intent on Larissa that he hadn't noticed the way she was plastered to Everett. He let her go and eased away, smoothing her covers as he went.

Larissa ignored the tingling sensation his touch caused, focusing instead on her son. "Hey, buddy." She opened her arms to him, as much as she could without sending her painful broken ribs into spasms.

As cautiously as Everett had, Owen slipped his arms around her waist. "Grandma says I have to be careful 'cause you're broken."

"Grandma," she repeated, her eyes swinging wildly to Everett. Had her mother been here?

"My mom," Everett explained. "She and Owen came to an agreement on what he should call her. I hope that's okay."

Larissa nodded, feeling dazed. How long had she been out? Long enough to get engaged and acquire a new grandmother for her son, apparently.

As if she knew she was the topic of conversation, Mrs. Honeywell poked her head around the door. "Is it okay if I come in? I don't want to intrude."

"Please come in," Larissa said, smiling. She was overwhelmed, but not necessarily unhappy. She liked Everett's family very much.

"I wanted to poke my head in and make sure you're okay," Mrs. Honeywell said. "And to tell you we couldn't be more thrilled to have you and Owen join our family."

"Thank you," Larissa said. The unreality of the situation hadn't yet worn off. She had no idea what else to say. Thankfully Mrs. Honeywell didn't seem to expect anything more from her. She was smiling at Larissa as if she truly was happy to have her as a prospective daughter-in-law. Larissa wondered if the older woman had forgotten she was talking to a Porter. "We'll see you tomorrow at home, dear," she added before turning to leave the room.

Once again Larissa turned questioning eyes to Everett. "You're going to be off your feet for a few weeks. I thought it would be better for you to recover at the farm so we can take care of you guys. And that will give us plenty of time to plan things."

"Okay," Larissa said. The dazed feeling was giving way to numbness. Was any of this real, or was she dreaming?

Everett stood. "My brothers are meeting me at your house to help pack and move your stuff. Owen is going to help." He bestowed an approving smile on Owen who wiggled like an eager puppy. "We'll be back tomorrow to pick you up." He paused uncertainly beside her bed, not sure if he should kiss her or simply leave. In the end he must have decided against the kissing.

"Sweet dreams, Larissa," he said instead. Then he walked around the bed and claimed Owen, laying a hand on his shoulder.

"Bye, Mom," Owen called without looking back. Larissa watched them walk out the door, looking so much like father and son it was uncanny.

I'm marrying Everett and moving to the farm. I'm actually going to be a Honeywell. Maybe it was the pain in her body, or the sudden confusing twist of events. Whatever the reason, Larissa burst into tears and cried herself to sleep.

CHAPTER 17

The next morning felt like a return to sanity. Had she actually agreed to marry Everett? And, if so, could she get away with blaming it on the morphine? What had she been thinking? She couldn't make a lifelong commitment to someone to save him and his family from a little bit of town gossip.

Her resolve wavered a few hours later when Everett and Owen arrived. Everett was so very handsome, and Owen was so very happy. In Everett he had found everything he thought had once been missing from his life. But still, she couldn't commit herself to a loveless marriage of obligation because it was what Owen wanted. She was a selfless mother, but not that selfless.

Then Everett smiled at her and leaned in to kiss her cheek. "How's my patient today?"

Wishing for a whole lot more than a kiss on the cheek. The thought popped out of nowhere, probably heating her cheeks with a blush. Suddenly she realized how she must look—unshowered, bruised, and wearing a hospital gown. No wonder he had gone for the cheek.

"Ready to get out of here," Larissa said. Owen grabbed the remote control and plopped into the chair beside her, turning immediately to the cartoon channel. How he knew which channel it was remained a mystery. They didn't have cable at home.

Everett perched on the edge of Larissa's bed and picked up her hand. "I have something for you." He slipped a ring on her finger and let it go so she could make her inspection.

She lifted her now trembling hand to her face, staring at the ring in awe. It was huge, more befitting a socialite than a cop. She would never be able to wear it at work, not only because she didn't want anyone to steal it, but also because she ran the danger of busting someone's face open if she got into an altercation. It was large enough to serve as a very expensive set of brass knuckles. Soon, however, the magical power of diamonds began to work on her, making her forget everything but how sparkly the ring was.

"It's so pretty," she said sincerely. She had never owned jewelry before, and certainly not something like this. "How did you get this between last night and this morning?"

"I didn't," Everett said. He glanced at Owen, but the room could have been on fire and Owen wouldn't have torn his gaze from the cartoon alien on the screen. "I bought it seven years ago." Everett's eyes turned back to hers, their black depths loaded with unspoken meaning.

Had he bought this ring for *her* seven years ago? That seemed to be what he was trying to tell her, but surely not.

"I brought it to the hospital with me," he continued, clearing up any misconceptions. "I wasn't sure if I was going to use it, but I wanted it handy in case. My plan was to ask you to move to the farm so we could help take care of you until you were out of high school and of age. And then..."

And then what? Larissa was on the edge of her seat. Had he intended to claim Owen as his from the beginning? Had he really intended to marry a messed up kid with a baby, to keep them safe? That seemed like taking the friendship thing to the extreme, even for Everett. Especially for Everett, with his I'm-never-getting-married-to-anyone policy. "And then what?" she prompted.

"And then you told me to get out of your life," he said quietly, not quite meeting her eyes.

"Everett, I'm sorry for that. I was…"

"It's okay, Liss," he interrupted, cutting her off. "You've already explained, and it wasn't your fault. I'm sorry I listened. I should have vetoed that idea and gone ahead with my original plan. It was a confusing time for everyone. But here we are full circle, the three of us together, and everything is going to work out the way it should this time." He smiled at her, and her heart melted.

Maybe he didn't love her the way she wanted to be loved, but maybe he didn't have to. Maybe she could love him enough for the both of them. For a few beats they looked at each other, smiling and holding hands. Did Everett feel the tension hovering between them? Or was it all Larissa's imagination? If he felt it, he did nothing to relieve it. Instead he glanced at Owen.

"I haven't told him yet. I figured that was your place. Or we could do it together."

Larissa nodded, hoping he didn't mean right now. Telling Owen would make everything real. She winced as the pain in her side woke up and began to make its presence known.

"What is it?" Everett asked.

"Nothing. I'm uncomfortable in this position, but it takes too much effort to move. It'll go away soon."

"I'll help you," Everett volunteered. He stood and gently scooped her off the bed. "Where do you want to go?"

Nowhere, Larissa thought. It was the closest he had come to holding her in seven long years. She wondered if he was having similar thoughts because he froze and stared at her unblinking, his face very close to hers.

"There's not much privacy at the farm, Larissa," he whispered. "Maybe when you're better, we can have a night out to celebrate."

Was he asking her for a date? "I'd like that, Everett," she whispered.

He smiled. "So would I." He set her back down so she was resting her weight on her other side, and then he let her go. The doctor arrived for his rounds then and declared that she was free. Owen seemed disappointed to have to leave the television.

"The farm has cable," Everett announced.

"Owen's not allowed to watch much television," Larissa said, feeling slightly frustrated at Everett's intrusion.

"He'll be so busy he won't have time for television. Horses trump cable any day."

"Everett, is it safe for him to work so closely with the horses?"

"Of course it is. It's the way my brothers and I grew up."

"Yes, but you're not my baby," Larissa said, shooting Owen a protective glance. He was little, and the horses were so big.

"I'm not?" Everett asked, his tone full of mock innocence. "I was hoping maybe I was."

Larissa's eyes settled back on him. Was he flirting with her? If his grin was any indication, then the answer was yes. She almost sighed. The man had the epitome of a heart-stopping smile, complete with lush red lips, perfect white teeth, the right amount of sexy beard stubble, and one elusive dimple.

"That's twice now I've made you blush—practically a record," Everett said.

"Be careful," Larissa warned. "Turn about is fair play."

"I'm not worried. I don't blush easily."

Larissa took that as a challenge. What could she do to make Everett blush? A nurse arrived with a wheelchair then.

"Let's get you dressed, hon, and you're free," the nurse announced.

"I can do it," Larissa said, embarrassed at the thought of someone else putting her clothes on, especially when she hadn't showered in two days.

"I think you might feel differently after you try," the nurse said. "Lifting your arms over your head isn't going to be easy for the next couple of weeks until those ribs begin to heal. Your husband can help you now if you want. He'll probably have to dress you at home anyway."

Larissa looked at Everett and noticed that his face was now very red, indeed. "I think I'll sit this one out," he said, standing. "And, for the record, there's a vast difference between a blush and a flush, little miss." He gave Larissa a pointed glance before exiting the room.

She laughed, wincing as Owen stood and followed Everett into the hallway.

The nurse was smiling, too. "How long have you been married?"

"We're not," Larissa said.

"Oh." The nurse glanced at Larissa's left hand.

"We're engaged," Larissa said, stumbling awkwardly over the unfamiliar words. *Engaged.* How long would it take to get comfortable with that concept? She didn't have long to ponder because the nurse hadn't been exaggerating. Getting dressed hurt. When it was over, Larissa lay back on the hospital bed, panting and exhausted.

The nurse left, admitting Owen and Everett on her way out.

"You okay, Liss?" Everett asked. He braced his hands on either side of her head and leaned over her as she lay sprawled perpendicular to the bed. Larissa couldn't answer; it took too much effort to breathe.

"Mom," Owen said uncertainly as his anxious face peeped over the bed.

Larissa forced a smile. "I'm fine, honey," she lied. Her eyes implored Everett to help her reassure Owen.

"Mom's fine, buddy," Everett said cheerfully. "She can't stand the thought of leaving this comfortable hospital bed. She doesn't realize her room at home is even better."

"It is, Mom," Owen said earnestly. "Wait until you see. And I have to show you my room, too. It's huge, and Grandma says we can decorate it any way I want." His happy chatter worked to pass the time until Larissa's pain ebbed back down to a bearable level. She wondered how long it would take before simple tasks were no longer excruciatingly painful.

"*Better?*" Everett mouthed.

She nodded.

"Ready?" he asked out loud.

"Ready," she said, sounding weak and half-hearted to her own ears. She started to sit up, but Everett stopped her by once again scooping her up and depositing her in the wheelchair. Once he had her settled, however, he realized his arms were trapped beneath her.

"Clearly I did not think this through," he said as he gently began to extract his arms, careful not to jostle her. "There," he announced when at last his hands were free. "Do you want a blanket or anything?"

She must look really pathetic for him to treat her like such an invalid. "I'm fine, Everett. Thank you."

"I wish I could ride in a wheelchair," Owen said. "That would be awesome."

Larissa could have told him all the ways it wasn't awesome, but she refrained. "You could ride in my lap," she suggested, and then she and Everett laughed at his horrified expression. Owen only willingly sat on her lap when he was injured or upset.

They were still laughing as they rounded the corner and ran smack dab into Calhoun Boyd. Who was holding flowers. For Larissa.

Instinctively she shielded her left hand, not wanting him to see her ring until she could try and explain. She thought she was being subtle, but Everett's great height gave him the visual advantage. His hands tightened on the wheelchair handles.

Calhoun, who had no idea why the air was suddenly cracking with tension, thrust the flowers into Larissa's lap. "These are for you," he said unnecessarily.

Owen, already wary of Calhoun after they met at his school, moved closer to Everett who reached out and laid a protective hand on his shoulder. Larissa wanted to crawl through the floor at the awkwardness of it all.

"Thank you, Cal," Larissa said. She hoped the warmth she infused in her voice would go a long way to cover the impolite coldness now radiating from Owen and Everett. Perhaps if she introduced them. "This is my son, Owen. I guess you guys had an unfortunate encounter yesterday at his school, but I wanted to thank you for trying to pick him up. That was so thoughtful of you. And this is Everett Honeywell. He's my..." She broke off, unable to complete the sentence. She couldn't do it; she couldn't tell this perfectly nice man whom she'd had a date with three nights ago that she was engaged.

What would he think of her? She'd allowed him to kiss her goodnight. How could she possibly explain that she had been nowhere near engaged then, that she and Everett had never even dated. What a mess.

Everett, though, had no such compunctions. "I'm her fiancé," he said, holding out his hand in a gesture that was supposed to be friendly but ended up looking challenging.

"Congratulations," Cal managed to mumble as he pumped Everett's hand. "Have you been engaged long?" His eyes flicked to Larissa, and she resisted the urge to squirm as she read his unspoken question. *Were you engaged when you let me take you out and kiss you goodnight?*

"No, actually, since yesterday. We've been estranged for, well, for seven years." He glanced at Owen. "But these types of situations have a way of making you realize what's most important. Don't you think?"

"Uh, sure," Cal said, clearly uncomfortable and dying for an escape. "Well, take care, Larissa. I'll let work know you're doing okay." He turned and practically sprinted away, bypassing the elevator in favor of the stairs.

Larissa felt horrible. She had hurt Cal, a man who hadn't dated since his divorce. A man who, despite outward appearances, was still emotionally fragile. She knew it must appear to him that she had used him to make Everett jealous—something she would never do. But how was she supposed to explain the truth?

I was raped at a party, and Everett's pretending to be Owen's dad to protect me. Oh, and I'm only engaged to him to try and protect him and his family. That wasn't the sort of information she wanted to share with anyone, and certainly not one of her coworkers.

They were silent and somber on the trip to Everett's SUV. He lifted her up, and she tensed when her ribs throbbed. Everett wouldn't look her in the eye, which was okay because she didn't feel like looking at him, either.

They were almost home when Owen spoke. "What's a fiancé?"

CHAPTER 18

No one answered until Everett pulled up in front of the house and turned off the car.

"Why don't you give me and your mom a chance to talk and then we'll explain everything," Everett suggested.

"Is it something bad?" Owen asked, apprehension in his tone.

Everett smiled. "I don't think so."

Owen nodded before opening the door and hopping down. Instead of heading toward the house, though, he turned and headed for one of the horse barns.

Everett let out a long, slow breath. "I need to know what's between you and that man, Liss."

"Nothing," Larissa said. Her first reaction was to tell him it was none of his business. Then she remembered it was now all of his business. He was her *fiancé*.

"Then why did you hide your ring?"

"Because I didn't want to humiliate the man I went on a date with by telling him that—oh, by the way, I'm engaged—when three nights ago he walked me to my door and kissed me good night."

"You kissed him?"

"Of course I kissed him, Everett. It was a date."

"Do you love him?"

She laughed over the absurdity of the situation. Here she was, sitting with the man she loved, the only man she had ever loved, and he was asking her if she loved a stranger. Once again she wanted to hold on to her anger, to ask him why he cared when he had never said he loved her. But then she saw the hurt and shock mingling on his face, and she couldn't do it. "Of course not. I barely know the man. We had one date, and he spent most of it talking about his ex wife. This was his first date since the divorce, and that's why I didn't want to hurt him. He's a nice guy, and he's in enough pain without me adding to it. I feel horrible."

"Lissy." His tone was soft and filled with remorse as he scooted across the seat. "I'm sorry. I wasn't trying to be a possessive caveman. This is all new to me, you know." He slipped his arm around her and eased her closer.

She rested her head on his chest and inhaled. He smelled amazing. He felt amazing. He *was* amazing. And, for whatever cosmic mistake, he seemed to want to be with her. Her arms slipped around his waist and clung. "Everett, I want…"

"What? Anything, Liss, and it's yours. Give me a clue, and I'll make it happen. What do you want?"

You. Love. A real marriage. A relationship of equals where you tell me your secrets, and lean on me for support. "I want a shower."

He chuckled. "I probably can't give you that, but there's a bathroom in your room."

She smiled, smoothing her hand over his chest while he did the same to the back of her head. "This is nice," he whispered.

She lifted her face, practically begging him to kiss her. For once he looked like he was going to comply, but before she could find out, the door opened and Owen hopped back inside.

"Grant says fiancé means you're getting married. Are you getting married?"

"Well, yes," Everett said. "Is that okay?"

"Okay? It's awesome!" Owen exclaimed. "Could I have a little brother, too?"

Larissa tensed, but Everett laughed. "Sure. As many as Mom wants." He turned to smile at her, and she felt herself blushing again.

That answers that question, Larissa thought, glad to know they wouldn't have a marriage in name only. The way Everett was so reticent to touch her, she hadn't been sure.

He reached over and lightly brushed her too-warm cheek. "That's three times. Let's get you into the house, future Mrs. Honeywell, before my family comes to get us."

He lifted her and carried her—despite her protests—all the way to her room.

"What's the point of being seven feet tall if you can't carry your girl around?" was his response when she told him she could walk.

That shut her up, and also brought another blush that she hid by pressing her cheek to his shoulder. He thought of her as his girl?

By the time they reached her room, she was exhausted. "I don't know why I'm so tired. I haven't done anything this morning."

"Your body's trying to heal, Liss. Give yourself a break." Everett set her on the bed and hovered, his hands braced on either side of her head.

Kiss me, kiss me, kiss me. Larissa couldn't have made the signal any clearer if she had broadcast it in neon on her forehead. But he stood there, looking at her.

"Everett, when you said we were going to have more kids, did you mean we were going to adopt?" She was probably blushing again, but she had to ask.

Everett laughed. Not a light chuckle of amusement, but a deep, belly-shaking guffaw. "No. I plan for us to make them the old fashioned way."

"Oh." She was definitely blushing now. "Okay."

He was still smiling. "I'm glad you approve of the plan. Get some sleep, Liss." He leaned down and kissed her on the forehead—*on the forehead.* Mr. I-want-to-make-them-the-old-fashioned-way apparently had a lot to learn about how that worked.

With that thought in mind, Larissa closed her eyes and drifted to sleep.

She woke an unknown time later with a pressing need to visit the bathroom, but that was easier said than done. Slowly, inch by inch, she eased herself to a sitting position and pushed off the bed before remembering it wasn't only her ribs that were injured. The memory came crashing back when she tried to put weight on her sprained ankle and it crumpled. She lunged for the bedpost, letting out a stifled scream of pain and her ribs wrenched. Where was her personal taxi service when she needed him? Not that she wanted him to carry her into the bathroom. Ick.

She decided to kill two birds with one stone. As long as she was going to the bathroom, she would take a shower. Since there was no suitcase in sight, she guessed the dressers must be filled with her clothes. She hobbled to one and leaned on it for support as she rifled through, looking for a shirt with buttons. Raising her hands over her head wasn't something she wanted to repeat any time soon. Only two of her shirts were the button up variety. Maybe she could borrow a shirt from Everett and wear it as a dress.

Even though she had been half kidding, the thought of wearing Everett's clothes was an intimate one. And the thought that they would soon be getting much more intimate than that was enough to make her want to bury her face in her shirt until the embarrassment went away. If only she wasn't so inexperienced when it came to men. Not counting whatever happened when Owen was conceived, she'd had exactly two kisses in her life—the first with Everett, and the second with Cal. And now she was going to be married. It was enough to make her hyperventilate. If it was anyone but Everett, she would be petrified. With Everett, she was merely nervous. He wouldn't hurt her or make fun of her for her inexperience. Who was she kidding? She would be lucky if she could get him to touch her with a ten foot pole.

Maybe he truly wasn't attracted to her. Gorgeous as he was, he could do much better. And she was six years younger. Maybe he still saw her as a child. If so, her wardrobe would do nothing to help that misapprehension. She tended to dress overly conservative, always paranoid someone might think she was promiscuous because she was a single mother. And then there was the undeniable little niggling voice in the back of her head that told her if she had dressed more conservatively seven years ago, she wouldn't have been attacked. Her shirt hadn't been tight or revealing, but the pants had been Angie's, and they had been snug. Maybe by wearing pants like that she had put off a vibe she wasn't aware of.

She gave herself a disgusted mental shake. Rationally she knew it wasn't her fault she had been attacked that night. But more often than not her emotions overrode her rationalization and she ended up blaming herself for her stupidity. She should probably have undergone some counseling or something, but who had time or money for that?

As she stood under the spray, she realized several things about the Honeywells' house. First, it was hands down the nicest place she had ever been. Both her room and Owen's had private bathrooms. And those bathrooms had what appeared to be marble countertops with fixtures that probably cost more than Larissa paid per month in rent. Not that the rooms were opulent or ostentatious—they were simply tasteful in a way that let the casual observer know this family had been in possession of wealth for a long, long time. Second, Larissa thought their hot water must never run out. She had been standing in the shower, her injured ankle held aloft like a flamingo, for what had to be twenty minutes, and the shower was still as hot as when she started. Everything was clean and beautiful and she never wanted to leave this place.

You don't have to, a little voice reminded her. *You're going to be one of them soon.* One of them. That was what her parents would say when she told them she was marrying a Honeywell. "You're going to be *one of them.*" And they wouldn't mean it as a compliment. How many times had she heard her family complain about the Honeywells? *I saw those Honeywells in town today. They think they're so great with their fancy cars.* Or, *I heard one of the Honeywell boys got arrested again. You know they're going to get off without a mark, not like Nick who didn't do anything wrong.* Larissa hadn't been able to keep her mouth shut on that one. She had pointed out—to her father, no less—that Nick had been caught red-handed trying to poison a horse worth a million dollars.

Predictably, her father had backhanded her across the mouth for both her insolence and her family disloyalty. And now she was going to marry one. How would that go down?

"Mom, Dad, meet Everett. We're getting married."

She could picture the stunned looks on her parents' faces. Would her father hit her in front of Everett? Not likely—not only because he would be too afraid of retribution, but also because her father hadn't hit her in many years. He was too old and too tired to fight much anymore. He hadn't even beaten her when she told him she was pregnant with Owen.

"Another daughter knocked up. So what else is new? We're not raising the brat. Find a new place to live," had been his only reply before he turned his attention back to the television.

Her mother's response had been almost smugness. *"I guess all those good grades didn't earn you much after all, did they, Larissa? See if one of your sisters will take you in. You'll probably have to give her your welfare money, though."* Then she, too, had turned her attention back to the television, and that had been the extent of Larissa's familial support during her pregnancy.

At long last Larissa made herself step out of the shower. Not because she wanted to, but because she was afraid to test the theory about the Honeywells' hot water supply. What if they ran out, and someone traced it back to her? *You were in the shower for* how *long?* was a question she really didn't want to face on her first night in her new house.

She pulled on the button up shirt—still no easy task—and a pair of loose-fitting pants, taking special care to ease them over her injured ankle. Her hair was a tangled, matted mess, but there was no way she could comb it on her own right now. Maybe she would find Owen and ask him to do it. He had a secret fascination with her hair, and often asked her to sit on the floor so he could brush it. Larissa thought it was cute, especially because he was such a guy's guy. Makeup was another lost cause, and she sighed, hating to greet Everett's family as fresh faced and young-looking as a schoolgirl.

She hobbled out of the bathroom and stopped short at the sight of

Everett sitting on her bed. He looked at her with a caught, guilty expression that quickly changed to one of disappointment. "You're dressed."

"Were you hoping to find me otherwise?" she blurted.

He cleared his throat and looked away. "The nurse said…never mind. Looks like you handled it." He looked back at her again with a pleasant smile this time. "Ready for supper?"

"I need to find Owen. My hair is a mess."

"I'm trying and failing to connect those two sentences."

"I was hoping he could comb my hair for me," she explained. "He does it sometimes. Don't tell him I told; he would be mortified."

"I can do it, if you want," Everett said, sounding almost shy.

"You know how to comb hair?"

"Insert comb and pull," he said, his shyness evaporating in the wake of his teasing tone. "Unless there's some girl trick I'm not aware of."

"No, that pretty much sums it up." She went forward and sat in front of him on the bed. For Owen, she sat on the floor, but Everett was so tall she didn't even have to duck. He took the comb from her and began detangling her hair. Larissa closed her eyes, enjoying the sensation. For someone with such big hands, he was remarkably gentle.

"I think we're done here," he whispered. Tentatively, he set the comb aside and rested his hands on her shoulders, withdrawing them almost as quickly so he could tuck them under his legs. "Do you need anything else?"

"Yes, but I can get someone else." She said it without turning around. Why didn't he like touching her? Granted she wasn't wearing makeup, but she was clean and good smelling now.

"Lissy, don't be crazy. I can help you. What do you need?"

She took a breath, forcing herself to say the words. "I need someone to rewrap the bandage around my ribs."

He paused. "Are you uncomfortable with having me do it? Do you want me to get Allie or Haley?"

"If that's what you want," she said, trying not to let her hurt show.

He raised his leg all the way over her head in order to move in front of her and look into her eyes. "What's going on here? What am I missing? If you want me to wrap your bandage, I'll do it."

"Are you sure, Everett? Because you don't seem to want to touch me." There. She said it. Now the dreaded cat was out of the embarrassing bag.

He blinked at her a few beats before he burst out laughing. If she was able to, she would have wrenched away from him. As it was, she gingerly crossed her arms over her chest and frowned. Realizing he had made her angry, he quickly sobered and wiped the amused grin off his face. "Sorry, Liss, I'm really sorry." Slowly, tentatively, he reached out and rested his hands on her biceps. "I'm laughing because you think I'm afraid to touch you when the truth is that I'm afraid I won't be able to stop touching you."

She wasn't sure how to respond to that. "Oh. Is that such a bad thing? I mean, we are engaged now." She bit her lip uncertainly, still not sure if he was going to reject her again.

He knelt on both knees and crawled closer. "You know what my family is like. They make the pope look morally loose by comparison, and I don't necessarily disagree with those values. It probably wouldn't go over well to, uh, break those stringent codes before we're married. Even though they think we've already lapsed and produced Owen, there's no free pass for what happens before we're married."

"Right, I get that, and I'm happy to abide by your parents' rules."

He smiled, looking relieved. "Thank you. While we're on this subject, I should also tell you that I've been holding back for another reason. I don't want to traumatize you."

"Traumatize me? From what I remember, you're a really good kisser. Unless something has changed, I think we're safe."

He laughed again, moving even closer until he was butted up against the bed and she was firmly in his embrace. "Thanks for that, though it wasn't what I meant. You were victimized at that party."

Borrowing some of his hesitancy, she tentatively slipped her hands between them, clutching his shirt to keep them in place. "I don't remember anything that happened to me, Everett. From the time I blacked out to the time I woke up, it's all a complete blank."

He looked enormously relieved at that. "I don't want to frighten you," he whispered, but even as he said the words, his head tilted in her direction.

"Please, frighten me," she whispered, leaning in slightly so that, unless he was absolutely stupid, there was no way he could ignore her blatant "kiss me" signal.

And this time he didn't ignore it. He kissed her, softly at first as his lips brushed hers in a gentle caress. But for Larissa, who had waited so long and loved him so much, it wasn't enough. She drew him closer, intensifying the kiss so that it went from sweet to explosive with no in between. She tightened her clutch on his shirt, and he moved his arms up so his hands were in her hair, and then she was leaning over the back of the bed when she broke away to yelp in pain.

He helped her sit up and then backed off, trying to draw a full breath. "Sorry," he managed to say.

"Who needs a chastity belt when you have broken ribs?" Larissa said, and Everett laughed.

"I'm really sorry," he said, in full control of his breathing now. "Are you okay?"

"The wrap helps. Are you sure you can handle this?"

"Sweetheart, I'm a Honeywell. I can handle anything."

She laughed at his bravado, and then laughed again when she raised her shirt, being careful to only expose her stomach. Still, Everett stopped and stared, openmouthed. "I thought women get stretch marks when they're pregnant." He reached out and gently traced his finger over her navel.

"Women, not teenagers. That's the beauty of being a child who has a child; your skin is still as supple as the baby you're giving birth to. I'm sure I'll get them with the next baby." She bit her lip again as she watched him swallow, his Adam's apple bobbing convulsively.

"That's a whole lot of nice-looking skin you're showing there," he commented.

"It won't be after you cover it with that bandage," she prompted.

He nodded dumbly, still not taking his eyes off her stomach as he moved in and began to wrap.

"Not too tight," she coached. "I still need to breathe."

"There," he said after a few minutes of concerted silence. "Easy as pie. Put this down now." He tugged her shirt out of her hands and pulled it down before sitting hard on the ground. When he wiped his perspiring brow, she noted his hands were shaking.

"I'm not sure you handled that too well, Mr. Honeywell," she teased. He looked like he was either going to tackle her or pass out from the effort of trying not to.

He shook his head, not even bothering to disagree. "How soon can we get married?" he asked, his voice tense and serious.

Larissa's smile faded. She hadn't yet come to terms with their engagement, and now he wanted to set a date? "I don't know," she faltered. "I definitely want to be well enough to walk down the aisle on my own and, uh, enjoy our honeymoon."

Everett groaned and lay back on the floor throwing his arm up to cover his eyes. "You're killing me, Liss."

She laughed, enjoying his misery a little bit. A little while ago, she had thought he wasn't attracted to her at all. Now she found out he was so attracted to her he was actually in pain. Of course, he was twenty nine and, to her knowledge, had never dated anyone. He was probably ready to marry anyone at this point. "Everett, have you ever had a girlfriend?"

He moved his arm aside and squinted at her. "I told you I didn't want to date anyone," he said, sounding half offended that she hadn't remembered.

"I guess that's why I'm confused. You've gone from not wanting to date anyone to wanting desperately to get married."

He sat up and smiled at her. "Things change. People change."

"I'm sorry," she said.

His smile fled. "For what?"

"For changing something about you that you didn't want to be changed. I mean, how many years now have you said you're never getting married? And then I come along with my messed up life, and —BAM—you suddenly have to marry me."

"Larissa, here's something for you to think about: I don't *have* to marry you. And I stopped saying I didn't want to get married seven years ago. Now let's go to dinner because we're already late." He stood, scooped her into his arms, and carried her to the dining room.

CHAPTER 19

*L*arissa felt like all the Honeywell ancestors were looking down on her with shame and disapproval. She had no idea the Honeywells dressed for dinner. Not that they were in tuxedos and cocktail dresses, but they were a far cry from her velour pants and flannel shirt.

Mrs. Honeywell wore a matching outfit with a gold necklace and matching gold earrings that screamed of tasteful elegance. Allie had worked at the law firm in Lexington, so she was still in a matching business suit. Haley was pregnant with her second baby, but still managed to look adorable in her flowing maternity dress. And even though Mr. Honeywell and the four brothers had worked in the barn all day, they were now wearing khaki pants and button-down shirts. And then there was Larissa, poor, stupid Larissa Porter who never quite fit in. To make matters worse, everyone was so impeccably polite and friendly that no one so much as glanced at what she was wearing. She would feel better if they would shoot her a few scornful, disapproving looks but, no, they had to smile at her as if she were the guest of honor.

Owen, the traitor, felt no discomfort at all. He had decided that not only should the elder Honeywells be called "Grandma" and "Grandpa," but that all the brothers and sisters-in-law were now "uncle" and "aunt," much to their apparent delight. Everett was oblivious to her discomfort, beaming at her as if she were his most prized possession as he occasionally reached under the table to rest his hand on her knee. Okay, that part was nice. But couldn't he see how totally she didn't fit in here?

Even the conversation was over her head. Allie and Brent were talking law. Haley and Mrs. Honeywell were talking about some upcoming social function. The remaining members of the family—including Owen—were discussing horses. The closest Larissa had ever been to a horse were the occasions when she had picked Owen up from the farm. And now she was supposedly going to marry a man whose family had been breeding horses since the Pilgrims set foot on Plymouth Rock.

One of these things is not like the other, Larissa thought. She had worked so hard to overcome her childhood, to climb out of the pit of despair the Porters had created, to give her son a better life. And now, irony of ironies, her son was thriving in his new environment while she was rapidly succumbing to a panic attack. It didn't matter that she had spent seven years building a life for herself and Owen. With this one family dinner, she was once again the snot-faced, scrubby little six-year-old whose teacher took one look at her and judged her for being a Porter. She saw her life stretching out before her, an endless array of nights like these as Larissa sat on the sidelines, feeling like an outcast. She couldn't do this. She absolutely, positively could not become a Honeywell.

"Liss, sweetheart, are you okay?"

Everett's gentle tone alerted her to the fact that she was clutching her fork and staring at nothing on the other side of the room. And now everyone else noticed and was also looking at her in concern. Great, just great. *Stare at Larissa the freak—free show, get it while you can.* She forced her fingers to uncurl from around the fork. Her mouth worked into a smile.

"I'm fine. Maybe there are a few lingering traces of morphine in my system." Great, now she sounded like a druggie. She should eat.

She should take a bite and chew, forcing herself to eat like a normal person who wasn't on the verge of running screaming from the room in abject terror. But she couldn't do it. If she tried to take a bite, she would no doubt choke.

"I'm actually not feeling too well," she said, which wasn't exactly a lie. Everything still hurt like crazy. Maybe that was part of her madness tonight.

"I'll help you to your room," Everett said. He removed his napkin from his lap, reminding Larissa that she had forgotten to place hers there, and causing her to turn three shades of red. How many times had she tried to impress upon Owen the importance of proper manners? And yet there lay her napkin—her cloth napkin— untouched beside her plate like any heathen.

"Don't carry me," she pled. She couldn't stand to draw any more attention to herself than necessary by being swept from the room like an invalid.

Everett nodded and put his arm around her instead, taking most of her weight so it barely hurt at all to hobble. When they were out of sight of the rest of the room, however, he did pick her up. And he didn't head toward her bedroom. Instead he grabbed an afghan from the den and headed outside.

"Where are you taking me?" she asked.

He didn't answer, but she had her answer when he sat on the porch swing and wrapped the blanket around her, tucking it tight and enveloping her with his big, strong arms.

And then, with no intention to start and no ability to stop, Larissa was crying. Everett held her, swinging them gently back and forth on a swing that would have been too tall for her, but fit him perfectly. She cried not only for tonight, but for all the times she hadn't fit in— and there had been many.

"Will it ever go away?" she murmured. "This feeling of not belonging anywhere?"

At first he didn't answer, but then she didn't expect him to. He was a Honeywell. How could he understand any of what she was feeling? And then he spoke. "Liss, I'm seven feet tall and the only introvert in a family of extroverts. Maybe you won't believe me, but I know a little of what you're feeling. And you do belong. You belong to me."

When he said it like that, so serious as his coal black eyes looked into hers, she did believe him. This time she didn't wait for him to kiss her. She kissed him, hoping he didn't mind the taste of her tears. He certainly didn't seem to, as he kissed her again and again and again. They sat on the porch for what seemed like forever, making out like teenagers. But the kisses were sweet and innocent and did more to seal the bond between them than any amount of words could have done.

Everett cupped her face as he kissed her, his fingers so large they spilled over into her hair. He made her feel cherished, beautiful, protected, desirable and innocent, all at the same time. The moment was so perfect she wanted to weep again, but she didn't. Crying meant she might have to stop kissing him, and she was nowhere near ready to do that. She wasn't sure she ever would be. And then her son's voice intruded questioningly from the doorway.

"Mommy? It's my bedtime."

She smiled, resting her forehead against Everett's cheek as she took a few shaky breaths.

"Want me to put him to bed?" Everett offered.

Larissa shook her head. Owen never volunteered to go to bed, so she knew what he was really saying was that he missed her, and rightfully so. The last few days were the most they had been apart since his birth. It had always been her and Owen, and now there was a whole new cast of characters to add into the mix. She wasn't sure how she felt about that.

"We can do it together," she suggested, wondering if Everett knew how monumental it was that she was including him in her private bedtime routine. No one had ever shared that ritual with her before.

"I'd like that," Everett said, his fingers feather soft as they skimmed her temple. "Owen, want to help Mom to your room?" he called.

"Okay," Owen called, always eager to be of service. Larissa realized then how much she appreciated the way Everett interacted with her son. He never condescended because he was young. Instead, he was always inclusive, giving him responsibility and making him feel invaluable. She realized something else too. Somewhere along the way he had stopped calling her "your mom" and instead started calling her "Mom" as if they were a real family.

Owen came out onto the porch and took Larissa's hand, putting his arm around her waist in the exact wrong place so that he jostled her broken ribs. Larissa wouldn't have complained, though, for all the money in the world. And especially not after he said, "Careful, Mom. Lean on me," so grown up and loving.

"You're a good man, Owen," she said, giving his shoulder a squeeze. He beamed up at her before quickly wiping his smile and clearing his throat. She could almost hear his thoughts. *Men aren't supposed to smile over junk their mothers say.* "You, too, Everett," she said, looking up at him. And though it was dim on the porch, she could swear he beamed at her exactly as Owen had done.

CHAPTER 20

$\mathcal{T}$hree weeks later, Larissa stood staring out her bedroom window. Her ankle and ribs were almost back to a hundred percent. She wouldn't be wearing heels or running a marathon anytime soon, but she was safe to go back to work—her doctor had said so.

But even if he hadn't, she would have gone anyway. She was going absolutely stir crazy. During the day when Everett was at work and Owen was at school, she was a prisoner of her room. And the odd thing about that was that there was no good reason for it. Mrs. Honeywell was usually gone. She served on the committee for several local charities, and she was otherwise very social, always lunching with friends or family members. She had invited Larissa on more than one occasion, but Larissa had declined. She felt guilty, of course, and hadn't wanted to hurt the older woman's feelings, but the thought of sitting at the country club with so many socialites staring at her in speculation was enough to send her into another panic spiral, something which had been happening more and more lately.

Allie worked a few days a week at a law firm in Lexington. When she was gone, she left her baby with a sitter, and those were the days

Larissa ventured from her room. She couldn't resist a baby. Babies didn't judge anyone.

For that reason she had also tried to visit Haley, but that hadn't gone well, either. Not that Haley was unfriendly. No, like all the Honeywells, she was sweet, welcoming, and practically perfect. But she was too much of a hands-on mom for Larissa to get much time with the baby. Instead, she had wanted to try and get to know Larissa, to bond over anything and everything she could think of. But she was two years younger, and all Larissa could think about was the time her little brother had punched Haley in the third grade, bloodying her nose before stealing her lunch and milk money.

Larissa didn't think Everett had any idea that she hid out in her room, skulking in the shadows like Howard Hughes in his latter days. She didn't want him to know, both because she was embarrassed about it and because things were going well between them. Even though he only worked a hundred feet away in the stables, he went in and came home at the same time, putting in a full and regular workday every day like clockwork. And every evening when he came home, Larissa was waiting for him, smiling as if she hadn't a care in the world. He greeted her the same way—with a kiss—and then talked to Owen, asking him pointed questions about his day at school.

She kept her happy smile in place during supper, playing the part of the well-adjusted Honeywell-to-be. After Owen went to bed, it was her special time with Everett, the time when she could really be herself and relax. With Everett, she could be herself—mostly. They talked about everything but what really mattered, like the fact that Larissa was miserable and teetering on the brink of an all-out break-down. Everett tried to get her to set a date for their wedding, but she put him off, usually with kisses that worked to distract him until they went their separate ways for the night.

Then she would lie in bed and try to drown out all the ghosts from her past. For the last seven years when she had been on her own, Larissa had functioned quite well. She never thought about her child-hood unless it was in a factual sense. No negative emotions had interfered with her every day life. She thought she was over it all. Boy was she wrong.

As it turned out, she had been stuffing everything deep down inside so that she could be the mother, father, provider, and caretaker that Owen needed her to be. Now in the cozy lap of luxury and emotional security that hallmarked the Honeywells' world, she was falling apart. Owen didn't need her for very much anymore. Now he had a bevy of aunts, uncles, grandparents, and even a father to see to his needs. It had only taken a few days before he gave in and started calling Everett "Dad." Larissa was surprised it had taken that long. He, at least, was having no trouble adjusting to their new situation. A friendly, social kid, he was soaking up all the extra company and attention, using it to fill the empty places Larissa hadn't even known existed in his life. Apparently he wanted a family; who knew? Everett did, and he was willing to provide it completely. They had already agreed that, after the wedding, he would officially adopt Owen and make him a Honeywell.

Larissa knew that she should be thankful her son wouldn't be growing up with the stigma of the Porter name, but like everything else lately what she should be feeling was far from what she actually was feeling. There was a small amount of resentment brewing inside her, and she didn't understand it at all. Why should she be anything but deliriously happy that Owen was going to have a father, a family, and a name? She wanted what was best for him, and the Honeywells were definitely what was best. What was *wrong* with her?

But now Everett was home, and she was once again the happy fiancée. She smiled and stood on her toes to receive his kiss.

"What did the doctor say?" he asked, his tone anxious. He had wanted to go with her, but she had put him off, needing the freedom to take a few deep breaths on her own.

"I'm all better," she said.

"That's great, Liss," Everett said, though he sounded mildly disappointed.

"What's wrong?" she asked.

"I'm going to miss wrapping you and helping you dress," he confessed.

She laughed. "Maybe sometimes we can do that for fun."

"Talk like that will get you married," he said, slipping his arms around her. Larissa's heart started to thud, but it had nothing to do with Everett's nearness and everything to do with his words. She had been putting off talk of their wedding until her doctor gave her the all clear.

"Supper's ready," she said. "Let's not keep your family waiting." She eased out of his embrace and turned toward the dining room.

Everett's sigh was loud and expressive. "You're going to injure that ankle again if you keep running away from me," he said.

She turned to smile at him over her shoulder, holding out her hand. He took it and caught up with her, giving her hand a squeeze. "You look especially pretty today," he said, noting her sleek black dress.

She looked down, giving herself a mental inspection, making sure everything was in its proper place. From her second night here, she had taken great care with her appearance, working hard to look appropriate, even though it meant near-excruciating pain as she lifted her arms to do her hair and makeup and wear clothes that had to go over her head. Everett, at least, had helped her with that part, delighting in his duty, asking her a few times a day if she needed to change.

"Thank you," she said.

"Is that new?"

She shook her head. "I bought it years ago for my college graduation."

"Do you have pictures? I would like to see them."

"I didn't end up going. There was no one to watch Owen." She tried to say it in a matter-of-fact tone, but it wasn't easy. That had been a hard day.

Everett slipped his arm around her. "We could have a redo. You could get your bachelor's, and then your master's. Maybe even your doctorate if you're so inclined."

She smiled up at him. "I'm not sure how that would fit into my work schedule, but it's something to consider for the future."

He stopped short, pulling her to a halt beside him. "What?"

"What what?" she asked.

"What work?"

"My work. I'm going back tomorrow."

"What?" he said, and this time he made no pretense of keeping his voice down.

"Everett," Larissa whispered with an embarrassed glance toward the dining room. "Can we talk about this later? Your family is waiting." There was no way she wanted to be the cause of delay for family dinner.

Begrudgingly, Everett consented, charging into the dining room like an angry bull while Larissa entered cautiously behind. Everyone at the table picked up on the tension, making conversation stilted and stressful. She picked at her food, always unable to eat when she was upset. Everett seemed to have no such trouble, but then maybe he did because he didn't take seconds. Instead he put down his napkin and excused himself and Larissa before leading her to her bedroom.

Once inside, he closed the door and turned to face her. Though he tried to soften his voice, there was no mistaking his anger, which seemed all the more vibrant because of his large size. Not that Larissa was afraid of him; he would never hurt her. It was simply daunting to face down that much angry male staring at her.

"What's this about you going back to work?" he asked, purposely keeping his tone low and calm.

"I don't understand why this is a surprise. You knew I would be going back after I was better."

He shook his head. "No, I didn't. I thought you were going to quit."

"Quit?" she repeated incredulously. "Why would I quit?"

"Oh, I don't know, maybe because some maniac almost killed you."

"He didn't almost kill me. In the scheme of things, he barely hurt me at all."

"Larissa!" Everett exclaimed.

"It's true, Everett. We had a scuffle and I received some minor damage. If you had seen how big and angry he was, you would know I got off lightly."

He closed his eyes and shuddered. "Don't say things like that to me." He opened his eyes and took a breath. "You don't have to work. I have enough money for you to stay home or go back to school or find somewhere else to work, somewhere that doesn't involve you being beaten."

"That was the first time in four years it's ever been that bad."

"But you've been involved in other altercations," he said.

"Not very often."

He swallowed hard, clenching his fists at his sides. "How am I supposed to live with the knowledge of what you do every day? All I can think of is the way you first looked in the hospital, broken and unconscious. You don't have to do this. Let me take care of you, provide for you."

Larissa could feel the panic rising in the back of her throat as the walls began to close in. She shook her head. "I'm not giving up my job. It's bad enough that we have to live here with your family; I'm not giving up my career, too."

Everett went deadly still at that. "What's wrong with my family?"

"Absolutely nothing," she said sincerely. "They're the kindest, most wonderful people I've ever known, and I genuinely like them. In fact, I'm convinced they're perfect."

"Why when you say it like that does it sound like an accusation?"

She pinched the bridge of her nose. How could she explain it to him when she didn't understand it herself? "I just...I can't do this, Everett."

"Can't do what?" he asked in that same cool voice that was both heartbreaking and terrifying. He was hurt and angry, a dangerous combination.

"This." She opened her eyes and looked up at him. "Everything. Being a productive member of a family that..."

"A family that what?" he asked as more anger than hurt crept into his tone.

"A family that's perfect," she said, willing him to understand.

He blinked at her, confused. "They're not perfect."

"They seem that way to me."

"I don't understand, Larissa."

"I know," she said. She couldn't expect him to understand when she didn't. She knew it was crazy and irrational, but it was how she felt. "I need a little bit of space, a little of my own identity." Though why she should want that she didn't know. All her life, she had run from being a Porter. Why was she so desperate to hang onto that now? "Work should help with that, and then I'm going to stop by and check on my house."

Anger flashed in his eyes again. "I don't understand why you won't let that place go. You don't need it anymore. Unless…unless you think you do need it. Is that what this is about? Do you not want to marry me?"

She paused too long before answering, but the answer wasn't as simple as yes or no.

"I guess silence is all the answer I need," Everett said.

"It's not…I just…" She drew a shaky breath, wishing he could see inside her heart, see all the love, confusion, and fear jumbled together. "Here," she said instead, wrenching off her ring and holding it out to him.

He looked at it. Maybe he did understand a little of what was going on inside her, or maybe he was too stubborn to give up yet. Whatever the reason, he shook his head and took a step back. "This isn't over yet. Put that back on, and we'll talk more tomorrow after you've had a chance to think."

She bit her lip, sliding the ring back on her trembling finger as tears dripped slowly down her cheeks. She wished he would hold her and tell her everything was going to be okay, that somehow she would work out all the crazy emotions jangling for supremacy, that they had a real chance of happiness together. Most of all she wished he would tell her that he loved her. He never had. She thought maybe he did, but it would be nice to hear the words, especially now when she needed them most.

He didn't hold her, though. Either he was too hurt, or too angry, or too uncertain. Instead he looked at her, a gut-rending expression on his face as he shifted anxiously back and forth. "We'll talk more tomorrow," he said.

She nodded, unable to speak.

"Do you want me to put Owen to bed for you tonight?"

She nodded again. She couldn't leave the safety of her room again tonight, not even for Owen.

"Goodnight, then," Everett said. He sounded as miserable as she felt. He turned and let himself out. Larissa crawled beneath the sheets still fully dressed and cried herself to sleep.

CHAPTER 21

arissa had expected to feel some sense of relief being back at work, but she didn't. She wasn't close to any of her coworkers. Cal was the closest thing she'd had to a friend there, and his stony silence and forced smile were reminders that she had messed that up royally. She wanted to try and explain, but there was no rational explanation for what had happened, and she had lost the will to try. Several people congratulated her on her engagement, but the expectant way they said it made her wonder if they were hoping she would fill them in on the mystery of how she suddenly became engaged to a Honeywell. If that were the case, they were bound to be disappointed. Larissa had no heart for gossip, especially when it was about herself.

The day was routine as she delivered civil papers and tried to arbitrate a couple of custody arguments. She felt cynical and impatient, wanting to yell at both parties to put their child ahead of their petty disagreements. Thankfully she had their court agreement right in front of her and simply had to remind them to follow it or else.

She found herself missing not only Everett, but the peaceful serenity of the Honeywell's farm, which proved how crazy she really was. She was miserable when she was there, and miserable when she was away; maybe she was plain miserable.

Tired and achy from her first day back, she almost skipped going to her rental house to check on it. But a flare of defiance made her decide to go. It was her house, and she had a right to keep it or do anything else she decided to do. When she pulled out her key, though, her hand shook on the lock. There was no sense of relief or welcome; instead the house felt like it belonged to a stranger. She stepped inside and stopped short. It smelled different, too. In fact, it smelled awful. Had the sewer backed up?

She took two steps into the room and stopped short at the sight of trash everywhere. Food containers littered the room, as did soda cans, beer cans, and toilet paper. There was only one explanation for how a room was this messy. Larissa looked through the piles of rubble, trying to spot her brother. And there he lay, curled on a pile of rags like a stray cat, dead asleep and covered in his own layer of grime. By the tracks up and down his arms, she knew he had been using heavily while he was here, and she finally figured out what the smell was, too. He had been cooking meth, right here in her house.

"Nick," she yelled, but he didn't move. Her heart started to thud. Was he dead? That had long been her worst nightmare, that he would overdose and she would be the one to find him. "Nick," she tried again, taking a step toward him.

This time he heard her, and he sprang up, crouching in front of his makeshift pallet like a dog guarding a bone. His hands were outstretched in full fighting mode, but he didn't attack. He remained crouched and breathing hard as he blinked at her, trying to wake up and clear his head. "Larissa?" he said at last.

"Yes, Larissa," she snapped. "Why do you sound surprised to see me in my own house?"

He stood shakily to his feet. His eyes were bleary and unfocused. He was high, but not euphorically so. Larissa guessed he was beginning to tweak as he came down from the high and began craving another. He was probably feeling pretty miserable, but that did nothing to lessen her anger. Instead, it only added to it. "You weren't using it," he said. There was no remorse in his tone. In fact, there was a whole lot of accusation.

"And you think that gives you the right to break in here like a common squatter and destroy the place? And you cooked meth here?" She enunciated each word. If he thought she wasn't going to report this, he was sadly mistaken. She had no patience for illegal activity, and especially not when it took place in her own house.

He shrugged. "What do you care, Miss High and Mighty Honeywell? I'm surprised you came down out of your castle to see the common folk. Oh, congratulations, by the way. Not that you told any of us you were engaged. We had to hear it from other people. I guess it's safe to say none of us will be invited to the wedding."

"You know what really makes me angry, Nick? It's that you break into my house, trash it, use it to cook illegal drugs and shoot up, and then somehow turn it around and make it about me because I got engaged. You're too high to understand how very messed up that is, but let me tell you it is."

"Whatever, Larissa," he said. "What do you care about this place? You could buy and sell ten of them now that you're a rich princess."

She gritted her teeth together. "Their money isn't mine. I still work for a living. As a cop, or did you forget?"

"Oh, no, I didn't forget. Perfect Larissa who never does anything wrong. Although, I guess you did one thing wrong. You got knocked up by a Honeywell. Or maybe you did something right. Cha-ching." His grin was ugly and made more so by his blackened teeth.

Larissa took a deep breath, trying not to let Nick get to her. This was the story of their lives—him pushing her buttons and her trying not to let it bother her. "If the worst you can say about me is that I made Owen, then that's not so bad, Nick. I love my son, and I love Everett."

All traces of a smile left his face then. "You would. He put me in juvie, but I guess that means nothing to you."

"You know that's not true," she said through gritted teeth. "You poisoned their horse and were about to poison another. You deserved to go to jail." There. She had said what she had been longing to for so many years. While the rest of her family had chosen to see Nick as a hapless victim of the Honeywell's wealth and influence, Larissa had known the truth, though she had never said as much to him before.

"Who cares about their stupid horses?" he yelled. "It's not like they don't have about a thousand more. They deserved what was coming to them and then some."

"Why do you hate them so much, Nick?" she asked. "They're kind and loving and, well, and perfect."

"That's why I hate them," he yelled. "Why do they get to have everything when we have nothing? It's not fair."

He sounded like a spoiled child, but Larissa was more disturbed by the resounding echo of agreement in her own heart. Had all those years of hearing Honeywell resentment somehow found a foothold? She shook her head. "They work hard, Nick. As hard as any people I've ever seen. All of them put in full days working in the stable, and not ordering people around. They shovel manure and all the other back-breaking work that it takes to make a business successful. Did you know Everett is an architect? He would rather be off somewhere designing grand buildings and houses, but he puts his own dreams aside to help his family. It's not some magical stroke of luck that makes them who they are. It's hard work and good choices."

"Gag," Nick said. "You've really been brainwashed, though I guess I shouldn't expect anything different from the sister who sold me out all those years ago. I know it was you who tipped them off about the horse." He tipped his head defiantly, daring her to deny it.

"You're right, I did," Larissa said, finally pushed past her limit of endurance. "And I would do it again any day and twice on Sunday. What you did was wrong, and I'm glad you were punished."

He flew at her, but she was ready. She sidestepped him, and he went down hard. But then he sprang back up again and took a swing at her. It was his standard right hook, and she easily dodged it. She almost felt disappointed. It would be kind of nice to have a good fight and clear her emotional cobwebs, but then that was a very Porter way of thinking. Violence was never the answer.

"Stop it, Nick, and get out of my house," Larissa said, but Nick didn't stop. She had underestimated how much of the meth was left in his system, but apparently it was enough to make his adrenaline surge because he kept advancing on her again and again and eventually his fists began to connect with her body. By the time Larissa realized this wouldn't be their standard matchup, she knew she was in real trouble. Nick, who was volatile and angry on a normal day, was high enough to be explosively angry. They were well matched in size and skill, but Larissa could usually take him—mostly because his attempts to hit her were usually half-hearted. He didn't really want to hurt her; he simply had trouble controlling his temper.

Today was different, however. This wasn't her brother, Nick. This was Nick the meth head who was still so out of his head that he couldn't keep a cap on his surging adrenaline. He was out for blood, her blood, and he was about to get it. Even though the man she had fought a few weeks ago had been much larger, she was more afraid now than she was then. Nick was wiry and ruthless. He could take a punch as well as she could—better because he was too high to feel it. And unlike the last time, no backup was coming. This was going to be a fight to the death between brother and sister, and Larissa had the sinking feeling she was going to lose.

They fought endlessly, rolling over and over on the piles of trash. A part of Larissa prayed she wasn't rolling over any used needles, but most of her brain was too intent on trying to stay alive to care about anything else. Nick was in a blind rage and beating her senseless whenever he could land a punch. Thanks to years of fighting with her brother, though, it wasn't often that he could get her to hold still long enough to hit her. The problem, however, was that Larissa wasn't in top condition. She was still bruised, sore, and exhausted. How long could she keep this up? Especially in light of the fact that Nick had endless energy, thanks to the meth.

While Larissa's strength was waning, Nick's seemed to be growing. At last he gained the upper ground, pinning her by straddling her chest, his knees anchoring her arms down. Instead of beating her, though, he grasped her skull between his hands and began slamming it into the wood floor.

"I hate you!" he screamed. "I hate you, I hate you, I hate you!"

She closed her eyes, not wanting her final image to be her brother's rage-filled face. It was ironic, really. She had lived her childhood in fear that one day her family's anger would go too far and they would kill her. Now she was an adult, finally out of their influence, and her brother was going to kill her.

Owen's face floated into view, followed quickly by Everett. At least she had the peace of knowing that Owen would be taken care of. Everett would follow through on his plan to adopt Owen. His family would continue to nurture and care for her son because that was who they were, and because they genuinely loved him.

Everett would grieve for her, and that made her sad. But what really hurt was the thought that a little relief might mingle with his pain. How could he not be a little bit glad to rid the nuisance from his life? Larissa was so messed up she couldn't even fit into a normal family when one was handed to her on a silver platter.

"Everett."

Had she said that out loud? Was she imagining his giant figure hovering behind Nick like an avenging angel? But, no, she wasn't imagining the way her brother flew through the air and smacked hard into the opposing wall. And she didn't imagine the way Everett knelt and cradled her gently in his arms. Though maybe she imagined the tears on his cheeks.

"You always come when I need you." Was that part out loud? She meant to say it, but wasn't sure her brain was connected to her mouth anymore. It certainly felt like everything was loose, including her teeth.

"Hold on, Liss," Everett said. "Hold on, baby." Somewhere outside a siren screamed. Had he called an ambulance? Everything felt so vague and hazy.

"I love you." She really hoped she actually said that, but there was no way to be sure. She tried repeating it over and over, the same way Nick had said that he hated her, trying to cover his messages of hatred with those of love. But then the edges of her vision started to fade, and for the second time in less than a month everything went black.

CHAPTER 22

*L*arissa woke in the hospital with Everett's head pressed to her neck again. He wasn't listening to her pulse this time, though; he was asleep. She brought her hands up and tangled them in his hair, drawing him slightly closer while she did a mental assessment of her physical condition. Her ribs were tender, but not any more than they already had been. The pain now seemed confined to her head, and it was intense. She closed her eyes, intending to go back to sleep, but Everett stirred.

"How are you?" he asked.

Better than you look, she thought. His face was ragged and haggard. She had no idea what time it was, but she knew he had to be exhausted. His beard stubble was longer than usual, and he looked pale and drawn. Before she could answer, though, he kissed her.

The kiss was sweet, tender, clinging, and laced with more than a hint of desperation. He finally broke away and rested his forehead on her cheek. "Liss," he breathed, and she heard it all in that one word— how terrified and upset he had been when he found her in her house. "You're really doing a lot to undo that whole calm, cool, and collected persona I had going." He cracked a smile, but she didn't.

"I'm sorry, Everett," she said sincerely.

He looked up at her, frowning because he read all that her apology implied. "For what? This wasn't your fault."

"Wasn't it? Then whose fault was it? I'm the common denominator in every catastrophe you've rescued me from."

"What are you talking about? I haven't rescued you from anything until today, and I'm glad I did. You have hairline fractures all over your skull. The doctor said if he'd hit you a few more times, then..." He swallowed hard, his Adam's apple bobbing.

"You've rescued me since day one," she said wearily. "You provided care and hope in my dark, lonely world. You were the one person I could count on, the one person who cared if I lived or died. You taught me how to be a good person, and gave me the assurance that I could one day amount to something. And now, with Owen, you've rescued me again."

"What does that mean?" he asked. He moved away from her and sat up, clearly agitated.

"Come on, Everett. The gig is up. For whatever reason, you've taken me on as a project since my childhood. Then I got pregnant and failed miserably, and you *still* didn't give up. You made up your mind to marry me and be Owen's dad, not even telling your own parents that he's not yours. Don't try and pretend this marriage isn't a rescue, because you know it is."

"Larissa, there are so many things wrong with that statement that I don't know where to begin. Let's start with your pregnancy. That wasn't a failure. It wasn't your fault."

"Then whose fault was it? I was stupid enough to go to that party when I should have stayed home and studied. I dressed up as if I were trolling for a man, and then I moronically took an open drink from a stranger. Even when it tasted funny, I convinced myself it was because it was diet. Then the next morning, when I woke up alone in a cheap motel on bloody sheets, did I call the police? No. I walked home, twenty miles. It took me most of the day, and when I finally got home my dad beat me senseless for staying out all night. Isn't that hilarious? The one time they actually try to enforce a rule had to be on that day."

"Stop," Everett said. His voice broke and he ground his palms into his eyes. "I can't stand this. I can't stand to sit here and listen to what you went through. Don't you understand that it wasn't your fault, Larissa? It was mine." His voice broke again, and when he wiped his hands on his cheeks they came away wet.

That shocked her so much she had no response at first. "What?" she asked at last.

"You were an innocent sixteen year old, so innocent you had no idea what horrible thing could happen to you by taking a drink from a stranger. I knew what could happen to you, but yet I left you alone and defenseless at that party, not even bothering to check and make sure you had a ride. And let's not go into the fact that I kissed you so inappropriately in the first place."

"You didn't kiss me; I kissed you," Larissa said.

"Then I kissed you back, and I shouldn't have."

They were quiet a few beats. "So that's what all this is about. You feel some misplaced guilt because of that party, and you're willing to marry me to make up for it."

He laughed, but the sound lacked humor. "If you weren't injured, I would be tempted to shake the sense into you. Why is it so hard for you to believe that I love you?"

"Because you've never told me," she said.

"I love you," he said, almost as an accusation. "And I knew it the moment I saw you at that party. You had your back to me. I looked at you, and it was as if the world flipped upside down and all my stupid proclamations about never wanting to fall in love became exactly that —stupid proclamations. Because I loved you, and I realized that maybe I've always loved you in some secret part of my heart. But you were sixteen, Larissa, and I was twenty two. Did you know that Allie grew up with us? From the very beginning, Corliss loved her. But he didn't touch her, not once until she was twenty two and out of college. So that's what I decided to do, only I knew I would never make it that long, so I decided to wait until you were eighteen and at least legal." He gave the humorless chuckle again. "And then I couldn't even wait two hours. You want to know something else? I didn't want to stop kissing you, either. If those people hadn't come along on the porch, then Owen *would* be mine. And as long as we're baring our souls, I should tell you that I was horribly jealous your whole pregnancy because I *wanted* him to be mine. I love you. I. Love. You." He put his hands on her shoulders and enunciated the words, making sure she understood them as he looked into her eyes.

His words brought no flood of reassurance and euphoria, though. "Why?" she said wearily. "What do you love most, Everett? My loads and loads of baggage? My proclivity for catastrophe?"

"Everything," he said sincerely. "Your intelligence and bravery, the fact that you've maintained a soft heart despite years of abuse, the way you are with Owen, the way you kiss, the way you look. I even love the way you smell, Liss. I'm hopelessly and totally addicted to you."

She was crying now, which was a shame because she wasn't a pretty crier. "Don't do this to yourself, Everett. I'm a mess. Walk away. Maybe if it was you and me and Owen, then things could work. But I can't be a part of your family. They're so great, and I…can't."

"I understand, Liss. I do," he reassured her when she looked doubtful. "I didn't get it at first, but I had some time to think about it last night. Your family wasn't the best. And my family is…"

"Perfect," she supplied.

He smiled. "They're not, but they're pretty great. It reminds me of this story I read about some people who were rescued from a concentration camp during *World War II*. They had been starved, surviving on a diet of a piece of bread and a cup of water a day. They were emaciated, skin and bones and barely alive. So their rescuers prepared a huge feast for them that night with every good food they could scrounge together. And the prisoners sat there staring at it in misery. Their bodies had become so accustomed to starvation that they couldn't eat. So finally someone had the idea to open a can of fruit cocktail and start feeding the prisoners little pieces. When that went down okay, they slowly started adding more food, little by little, until the prisoners could eat like normal and weren't starving anymore. I didn't realize how overwhelming it would be for you to join my family like that. I think we need to find a way to go back, to start with some fruit cocktail."

"I love them," Larissa interjected. "I really do. They're wonderful, and they've been so great to me and Owen. You can't imagine how horrible I've felt the last few weeks, how ungrateful."

"I know it, Liss. We need to ease you in slowly. I get that now. From now on, you and Owen can live on your own until we're married. We'll start with once a week family dinner and work our way up from there."

"And after we're married?"

He smiled because she hadn't said she wouldn't marry him. "I've had plans for my dream house floating around in my head for a while now. It's about time I build it. There's no law that says all the Honeywells have to live in the same house."

"I don't want to take you away from your family, Everett."

"You are my family, you and Owen."

"How can it not bother you that I'm a Porter?" Larissa said, incredulous. "My own brother tried to kill me, for goodness sake."

Everett put his hand over his eyes. "I am so freaking tired of hearing you say you're a Porter. Do you think I care? Because I don't." He dropped his hand from his eyes. "What can I do to prove that to you, Liss? Do you want me to take your name and become a Porter myself?"

Larissa blinked at him in surprise, not because of the last thing he said, but because of the first. A little known fact about the Honeywells was that none of them cursed. For Everett to say "freaking" was tantamount to saying a nasty expletive. "Potty mouth," she accused. "Since I've come back into your life, you've lied and said 'freaking.' And you think I'm not a bad influence on you."

He laughed, this time with amusement. He moved close and took her in his arms. "Clearly I'm on a path to destruction. Marry me and save me from myself." He kissed her, and it was a while before they talked again.

"Would you really take my name?" Larissa asked when the kiss finally ended.

"Of course not," Everett said. "I love you, but I'm still a man. I was trying to make a point, the point being that I wouldn't care if your last name is Hitler. I love you. Though I don't think we'll be having Nick over for dinner very often when he gets out of prison." His arms tightened as he frowned.

"I don't want him to go to prison," Larissa said. Strangely, she felt more mercy for him than she might have before she got engaged and moved in with the Honeywells. Previously, she hadn't had any compassion for Nick because she thought she had gotten over their childhood and he should do the same. Getting engaged had shown her she still had her own fair share of emotional scars. Nick was dealing with things the only way he knew how, by drowning his sorrows in drugs and alcohol. "Juvenile detention did nothing to help him, it only made him worse."

"I think it's out of your hands, Liss. He broke a whole bunch of laws, not least of which was trying to kill you."

"I want him to get some help," Larissa said.

"Maybe we can talk to the judge at his sentencing," Everett suggested.

"While we're on the topic of my family, I still have to tell them we're engaged. That's probably not going to go over well. And I have to warn you that they're going to take Nick's side. They're going to blame us that he was arrested."

His jaw popped and his hands clutched even tighter on her back. "Okay," he said. "We'll handle it together."

"There's one more thing. As crazy as this sounds after what I told you, I want a small wedding, and I want to invite my family. I don't want my dad to give me away because that seems like a lie, but I do want them in attendance. They're part of me and Owen, and it would be nice if our families could make peace. And by that I mean it would be nice if my family could get to see yours in person and realize they're not robber barons out to steal from the little people."

"I'll invite them personally if you want," he promised.

"No, you don't have to do that. But you do have to break the news that there won't be any alcohol at our wedding. Good luck." She paused, trailing her finger absently over his chest. "About my job…"

"I learned my lesson, okay? My sisters-in-law and mother read me the riot act after you left this morning. I know I can't ask you to quit a job you love because it will make me feel better. I'm scared to death that you're going to get injured again, but I'll suck it up and be supportive because it's important to you."

"Actually, I was going to say that I want to quit. I became a police officer because I wanted to make a difference, but I'm not sure I do. I think I would like to do something that can reach kids sooner, like teaching. I want to work until we're married, and then I want to go back to school." She chanced a peek at him and saw that his smile looked more encouraging than triumphant.

"I think that sounds great, Liss. And this time when you graduate college, you'd better believe the rows will be lined with family waiting to congratulate you."

&.

And three years later when Larissa graduated with her bachelor's degree, the Honeywells filled up two entire rows of seating to cheer her on. Even Ivy, Coy, and their kids came in from Montana for the occasion.

The Honeywells weren't the only ones in attendance that day, however. Larissa's parents sat beside Mr. and Mrs. Honeywell, looking uncomfortable and out of place. She thought Everett probably had something to do with getting them there, but he wouldn't admit it.

"They're your parents, Larissa. They love you and they're proud of you," was all he would say. They didn't tell her they were proud of her —or say much at all— but they were there, which was more than she ever expected.

She accepted her diploma and looked out on her family, the Honeywells who had made her one of their own despite her reservations, Owen, who, at ten, was taller than her, and her parents, who looked like they were ready to flee as soon as the ceremony was over. Larissa's gaze was automatically drawn to Everett. Her husband sat head and shoulders above everyone else, their four month old daughter in his arms.

"*Love you,*" she mouthed.

He smiled. "*So freaking proud,*" he mouthed in return.

And then she hurried off the stage because no one would ever understand why she was laughing out loud.

Thank you for reading *Wild and Unbroken,* the fourth book in the Honeywells of Kentucky series. For more books, please check out my website at www.vanessagraybartal.com